CHRISTMAS AT THE RIVERVIEW INN

MOLLY O'KEEFE

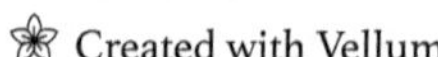 Created with Vellum

LETTER TO READERS

Christmas at the Riverview Inn is a looooooong time coming. I have been meaning to write Cameron's story for YEARS. And for the readers who have been patient - I really do appreciate it.

I wrote this book during the beginning of this quarantine - when days seemed to last so long and this whole thing felt a little bit like an adventure. It was fun to imagine a snowstorm and a country lodge and being alone with the love of my life with a bottle of wine and a cheese tray. Instead of being NEVER alone in my messy house with two kids and dog who somehow kept getting fleas!

I am more than ever so grateful to the escape that romance offers - as a reader and a writer. This was a very special book to write during a really wild time. And I hope you all enjoy it as much as I did.

For the beautiful cover I need to thank Mayhem Cover Creations. For copyediting - Judy Sturrup. And for brainstorming help, content editing, zoom chats, phone calls, long-distance wine and constant steady support and friendship - all my love to Skye, Annika, Simone and Steph.

And to you - my very favorite readers in the world - thank you. Stay safe.

If this is your first visit to The Riverview - pick up these other books:

Wedding at The Riverview Inn (Gabe and Alice)
Secrets At The Riverview Inn (Max and Delia)
Home To The Riverview Inn (Jonah and Daphne)
and preorder Second Chance At The Riverview Inn

1

———

7 Years Ago—August
CAMERON

It was the night of Josie Mitchell's high school graduation and she was drunk as an adorable skunk.

And Cameron was in the tenth circle of hell. Did hell have that many circles? Whatever, he'd found a new one. Charting undiscovered hell territory—of course he'd be good at that.

"That was a great night," she said, looking up at him from the passenger seat of his car.

"I'm glad you had fun. Do you...need help?" He opened the passenger side door to help her out.

"No," she said indignantly, and then all but fell out of the car.

"Okay, I gotcha," he said, getting her to her feet and propping her up against the front fender. Where she slid, like she had no bones, toward the front wheel.

"I had fun because of you," she said. "You made it possible, Cameron."

"Well..." He didn't know what to say to that so he let the

word trail off, grabbed her by the waist, and shut the passenger door. The sound of the slamming door sent some animal scurrying off in the bush and he hoped he hadn't just woken up the whole family.

"You give the best gifts," she said, turning to look at him, which meant her face was very close. He could turn his head and...

Do not turn your head.

His graduation present to her had been chauffeur service for her and her friends from the Riverview Inn—her family's lodge in the Catskill Mountains—to all the graduation parties. So she could have fun and be safe.

"Well, you're no slouch either," he said. The only way he knew how to take a compliment was to deflect it.

"Okay, five questions," she said.

"Josie."

"No. It's my turn. You five question me all the time."

"Fine. Go." He pretended to be annoyed. But mostly he was just nervous, not sure what questions might come out of drunk Josie's mouth. This was a game they'd started playing the summer the ground had been broken on Haven House. Top five favorite movies. Top five favorite television show finales—those were her type of questions. Top five ways to eat potatoes. Five worst things you've ever eaten—those were his.

"Best gift you ever got?"

"The coffeemaker you got me on my birthday." It was this high-tech, expensive camping thing that fit in the palm of his hand. He loved it so much. He loved that she knew he would love it. "But the year you got me all the Bourdain books. That was a good year, too."

"I need to replace those. You've read them to pieces

and..." She paused. Hiccupped. They stopped, a stone clattering off his shoe.

"Are you going to throw up?" he asked.

"Totally not," she said like she was offended. Which meant there was a fifty-fifty chance she was going to puke. He got them walking again. A little faster now.

Tonight, all he'd done was drive her and Helen around playing Beyoncé at top volume. He'd wanted to take her camping, to this place he'd found way up in the mountains behind the lodge, where there was a lake so clear and blue it looked like a sky. A place he knew she would love. But then he'd thought about being in a tent with her and rejected the idea.

He'd thought this would be better.

Stupid me.

"You are such a good guy," Josie breathed. Her breath was, like, eighty percent alcohol; he was getting drunk just being close to her. "Did you know that?"

"Yep," he said, trying to keep her on her feet and also open the back door. But she kept melting. Against him. Against the door. She was a puddle of Josie, in the way of everywhere he was trying to be.

"No." She grabbed his face.

Ouch. A little rough, there, Jos. And he thought she might be going for some kind of stern look, some kind of serious *I mean business* type look. But she was too drunk. And too dear to manage it.

God. She is beautiful.

As quickly as he thought that, he stopped. He was good at that after all these years. Thinking a thing he shouldn't and then just...not. Just stopping.

"You're my best friend," she said.

"I know."

He got the door open, managed to get them inside the dark and cool kitchen. No one there, waiting up.

Thank God.

But they were all sleeping here at the lodge. Alice and her husband Gabe. Max and Josie's mom, Delia. If they weren't quiet he'd have a million Mitchells in here.

"Cameron," she said. "You have to listen to me."

He actually laughed. "Josie. I'm listening. I'm a good guy and I'm your best friend. You're mine, too." These were things they didn't actually say out loud. Like saying them out loud might tip the chemistry of their friendship into that place he was trying to avoid. Trying not to look at. Trying to pretend didn't exist.

And, frankly, pretending was easier when they weren't touching.

He stepped away, setting down his bag, and she leaned back against the wall looking... *Jesus.*

"You need to drink some water," he said, and quickly turned away to get her a glass.

"Cameron," she said. "You could do literally anything. You know that, right?"

This again. "You Mitchells are really into telling me that these days." It was like they were trying to get rid of him. He'd turned twenty-two and suddenly his future was all anyone wanted to talk about.

Which was weird, because in so many ways he still felt like the shitty sixteen-year-old kid he'd been. He'd skipped school and gotten caught stealing a car and no one at home had given a shit. He'd been surprised the judge had—and had sent him to the Riverview for community service with Max instead of to juvie.

Max, Josie's adopted dad, had been his first boss here. But then he'd met Alice, who was in charge of the kitchens, and he'd traded Max and constant wood chopping for Alice and the kitchen. And it changed his life.

But years later, he still didn't know what he was supposed to do without the Mitchells. Alice. This kitchen.

Josie.

"Another one of my five questions. I still have some left."

"Not really."

She ignored him. "What do you want to do with your life?"

This. Right now. The Riverview Inn kitchen and you. Every day, all day.

"What do you want to do?" he asked, deflecting again. His great talent.

"Write amazing television. I want to make people cry. And change people's minds. And make them stay up all night to just watch one more episode." He smiled at her passion. "But the question is for you," she said.

His silence was possibly damning. But if he opened his mouth, the words he could not say would come out. *Love you.*

"You are smart. And funny. And you work hard and you're a great chef."

"Thanks, Josie," he said and brought her the water. "I'll put you down as a reference if I ever get another job." She took one gulp, most of which splashed down her neck, and handed the glass back. He ignored the water dripping across her chest into the top of her dress. It was yellow and short. She looked amazing in it.

"You...you could come to New York with me. You could get a job in a kitchen. Alice would give you a letter of recommendation and I'll go to school. And we'll be broke, but it would be fun? Wouldn't it? You and me? The big city?"

The words were quiet but they went through him like

arrows. Piercing his brain. His chest. His dick. He was embarrassed even thinking that word around her. But he couldn't stop.

With you how? he wanted to ask. *As your boyfriend? As your friend?*

Again, after long, long, looooong practice, he thought the thought and put it away.

"That's more than five questions," he said.

"Cam—"

"Let's talk about this in the morning," he said and smiled at her. "You need help getting upstairs?"

Please say no. Say no. Please.

He'd touched her more on the way from the car to the house than he had in years, and the whole left side of his body was raw and electric, and his dick was half hard. He felt like an animal *and* the luckiest guy in the world.

"I'm fine," she said, and pushed off the wall, overcompensated and nearly fell into the stainless steel table in the center of the room.

"Sure you are. Come on."

Girding himself, trying, like it was even a thing that could be done, to remove all sense of feeling on the side of his body touching her, he put his arm around her back and lifted her until she was standing.

"Hi." She smiled at him and his heart bobbed.

"Hi."

He walked them through the dark kitchen into the big main room with its fireplace and the wall of windows. Moonlight slid in great blocks across the floor, making their skin seem ghostly.

Cameron was painfully, excruciatingly aware of Josie's body against his side. The press of her leg. Her arm around his shoulders. He could smell her. Summer night and sweat and whatever sweet thing she'd been drinking. Something with cherries, probably. And green Jell-O shots. If he kissed her she'd taste like an artificial fruit salad.

When he'd had this brilliant chauffeur idea, he had not considered this. This being alone with her. Soft and pliant and happy and smelling so sweet. He had not considered the hell of the bright red filaments of her hair stuck to his neck in the heat.

And he knew it had never occurred to him because he'd gotten so good at not noticing this stuff about her. Because he'd done everything in his power the last year to not be with her like this. To be just friends.

Not touch her.

Not be close enough to smell her.

Or feel her.

Not think of her pretty eyes or the way she looked when the sun hit her just right. Or how her laugh, when she really got going, was like a gong that echoed through his whole body.

And now she was drunk and he felt like an absolute asshole because he was absolutely soaking it in. Like he could not get enough of her skin on his.

Dude. She's drunk.

There were plenty of people in his life, in this town, who thought the worst of him because of his mom and dad. Who wouldn't be surprised if he groped a drunk girl. But the Riverview folks—Alice and Max, they believed the best of him.

Max had even said it to him before Cameron left with Josie that night. *I trust you with my daughter.*

Cameron wasn't going to betray that trust. Ever.

So he tried, as best he could, to put distance between them somehow.

Up the stairs. To her room. Goodnight and get the hell out of here, man.

"Cam." Her voice was low as they made their way toward the stairs. "I need to tell you something..."

"Yeah?" he asked, trying to shift her just a little. He could feel the sweat on the insides of her arms and it was so far from gross, he wanted to run his hand from her wrist to her elbow, gathering all of it in his palm. He wanted to lick his hand.

He wanted to kiss her shoulder and taste her. God. He wanted to taste her.

"I love you."

The words sent sparks through his body and everything he felt for her—all the pent-up shit he'd been dealing with since she was a kid—it was dry kindling. It was explosives. A barn full of fireworks.

He laughed, ruthlessly stomping out the spark. "All right, drunky. You love everyone."

They made it to the first landing and he braced her against the wall, getting away from her as best he could.

"No," she said, grabbing onto him. Her hands clutching his shirt. His arm. "I mean, sure. But... " She took a deep breath. "I love you especially."

He turned his face away. Cameron didn't pray. His mother did and he saw how that had gotten her a whole bunch of nothing. But right now he prayed for the strength to say no to this.

I trust you with my daughter.

"Do you think of me...like that?"

All the time. Every minute. You would be horrified to know what I think of you. You would blush so hard you'd just be ash. And saying it out loud would make me blush so hard I'd be ash.

"Josie. You're drunk. Let's not talk about this now." He

pulled her off the wall. The room she liked to use in the lodge was three doors down. Fifty feet. If that. He just needed to get her into her room and himself away from her.

Pulled by him, she stumbled forward, colliding with his body.

"Careful," he murmured, trying to keep her upright. And then she did the impossible. The disastrous. She grabbed his face. Forced him to look at her. Right at her.

Growing up, he hadn't believed in love. There had been no sign of it in his house. No proof that it existed. After coming here it had taken some time to believe that all this love the Mitchells had and tossed around like it was all so easy was even real. It felt, at best, fake. At worst like a trap. And he'd believed for as long as he could that every single Mitchell was a sucker.

But then Alice had won him over.

And then Max.

And Patrick.

The rest of them.

But it wasn't until Josie that he'd believed in real love. The kind that changed the way his body worked. And his brain thought. The kind that opened up an idea to him he had never had the guts to think about.

Cameron wasn't cheesy, and he would never say it out loud, but he believed that he and Josie were as close to soul mates as two people could be. It was the only way he could explain not just what he felt for her, but the long and strange and totally unlikely road that had brought them together.

A thousand near misses and different decisions, and they never would have met.

"I've loved you for so long," she whispered. And she kissed him.

It was every single thing he'd ever wanted. And he gave himself just one second. One impossible taste of it. He allowed his hands to touch her hair. His body to register the feel of her against him. He was an absolute asshole but he kissed her back.

He kissed her back hard.

She moaned and he could taste the booze on her, and he hated himself.

She's drunk. This is not consent. It's not anything but drunk.

He pushed her away.

"Josie, you are drunk and now..."

She tried to kiss him again and he stepped back.

He watched her face go white and he realized she was embarrassed. That she thought he was rejecting her because he didn't like her. Didn't want to kiss her or touch her.

When that's all he'd wanted to do for so long now.

"I'm sorry," she whispered and started down the hallway.

"No, Josie. It's not like that."

"This is embarrassing," she said, pulling her hand away when he grabbed it. "Just...let me be embarrassed."

"Don't be embarrassed. Come on. You're drunk, Josie."

"Well, drunk was the only way I could do this, so...whatever."

He took a deep breath. Because he understood that. Needing the fake courage to break through the walls of their friendship. Of their age difference. Of being a kind of pseudo family.

And the truth was—he might never have made the first move. He'd been telling himself for a year he was just waiting for the right time. But now she was *leaving* leaving. For New York City and college.

Drunk and messy may not have been his plan, okay. But

this was the start of something. Something they could talk about tomorrow. Figure out—tomorrow.

She'd gone into the room and was struggling to take off her sweater.

He was not—no matter what—going to go in there and help her.

"Josie."

"What?" she snapped and turned to face him in the doorway. "What do you want?"

"I have waited a year to tell you how I feel and I won't be bullied into doing it when you're drunk."

She sucked in a breath and held it.

"How do you feel?" she whispered.

"Your five questions are up," he said with a smile. "We'll talk about it tomorrow. When you're sober and you feel like roadkill."

"This isn't funny, Cameron. I love you. I have loved you forever."

Oh, she was crying. And this shouldn't be sad. This was good. What was happening right now was good. But Josie crying was his kryptonite.

"Hey." He broke his rule and came into the bedroom. He lifted his hand, reaching for her face—so he could wipe away her tears. Because this beautiful girl should not be crying. Not today. "It's okay, Josie. Let's talk tomorrow."

She threw her arms around him and aimed her mouth at his, but ended up just under his nose. A little correction and she was kissing him again.

He could feel her heart pounding against his chest and he was sure she could feel the hard press of his dick against her hip.

He pulled away, and she stumbled and then overcorrected and fell sideways onto the bed, and since her hands were wrapped up in his shirt he went with her. He braced himself on an arm, so he didn't land on her. But their faces were inches apart.

She kissed him again.

He'd lived for so long locked inside the rules he had for his feelings about Josie and now they were everywhere. Like when the chickens got out of the run over at the farm. And everyone ran around trying to catch the damn things, which seemed somehow to multiply every second they were free.

As she kissed him, his feelings were multiplying. There were so many he was overrun.

He leaned back, pulling himself away from the never-ending temptation of her.

"Josie, I'm leaving before this goes any further."

"Sure you are," she said with a smile and then leaned up to kiss him again. He could feel her spread her legs. And he was aware, though he was trying hard not to be aware, of the fact that her skirt had ridden up. And she was very nearly naked from the waist down.

Yeah. This is over.

He put a hand on her leg. "Josie. Stop—"

She kissed him and he felt himself melting. His hand sliding up her leg.

"Cameron?"

It was a voice out of a nightmare. It was the voice of the worst possible person to witness what was happening. It was the voice of the only man whose opinion of him mattered.

I trust you with my daughter.

Cameron scrambled up off the bed and practically flew to the far side of the room.

Max stood in the doorway.

Cameron had seen Max mad plenty of times. When he

first got to the inn, he'd made a point of pissing the man off. But this...the look on his face. The rage and the disappointment.

Oh god.

And there was nothing Cameron could say. He could say he was trying to stop. He could say it wasn't going to go any further and he was just making sure she got to her room safely. But the fact that Max had caught him lying on top of his seventeen-year-old daughter, Cameron's hand on her leg—all while she was clearly drunk. And mostly naked...

Cameron had never been so embarrassed. Never been so angry at himself.

Josie sat up—she was saying something, probably trying to explain, but she was drunk. And it didn't matter. And then she gagged, and out of instinct Cameron stepped forward to help her.

"No," Max barked and lifted his hand like he would step forward and stop Cameron from touching Josie. And Cameron stopped, and then, because he couldn't stand the look on Max's face, he closed his eyes. And even that wasn't enough.

He'd see that rage and disappointment his whole damn life.

"It's not...what it looks like," Josie said. She stood and her skirt fell down around her legs, and Cameron imagined she tried real hard to look sober, but then she bolted for the garbage can and started to throw up everything she'd put in her body over the course of her night.

"Why don't you come outside with me, son," Max said.

"I can't leave her like this," Cameron said, imagining all those rock stars who'd passed out, thrown up, and ended up choking to death.

"I've got her," Delia, Josie's mom, said, tying up her robe as she came sailing into the room.

There, Cameron thought. *They don't actually need me.*

He caught Max's eye and wished more than he could say that the floor would open up and swallow him. It was alarming to realize he would quite literally rather die than talk to Max.

"Come on," Max said.

But the floor didn't open up and he had no choice but follow Max out of the room and down the hallway and stairs into the kitchen.

Where Alice was standing, spreading cheese over tortilla chips, taco meat, and beans in a pan.

She's making me nachos, he thought. Which meant she'd been planning this. A late night thanks for the gift he'd given Josie. It was so late and she was making him his favorite.

"Hey! The chauffer brought her home safely," she said with a smile, but with one look at Max's face the smile dropped. "What happened?"

Max blew out a long breath and looked over at Cameron. He was scared to open his mouth in case the ball of sick in his stomach came out.

"Somebody better say something right now," Alice said.

"I kissed Josie," he blurted.

"Oh, well." Alice looked at Max. "That doesn't seem so bad."

"We were on her bed and her skirt had gotten pulled up and my hand was on her knee."

"That sounds worse."

"She's very drunk," Max finished.

"Oh no," Alice breathed. "Oh..."

"I know what it looked like," Cameron said. "I do. And I

can't change that. And I know I made a promise to you but..." He ran out of steam. "It wasn't going to go any further."

Her saying yes while that drunk wasn't a yes at all, he knew that. Alice and Max had *taught* him that.

"You don't believe me." It wasn't even a question and he couldn't even blame them. If he'd walked in on some asshole on top of Josie like that, he'd have killed them. Straight up.

Max and Alice shared a quick look.

"I believe him," Alice said quietly. "I know the kind of guy Cameron is, and you do, too."

"You didn't see it," Max growled. "And as a cop I saw the aftermath of that way too often."

Oh god, he was lumping Cameron in with rapists. Abusers. Guys who took advantage. Assholes who hurt girls.

Am I that guy? he wondered. Did it matter what he thought when Max seemed so sure?

"I'm so sorry," Cameron said, and he felt sudden tears in his eyes. He grabbed his bag and his keys. "I'll go."

"Stop," Alice said. "Cameron, stop."

He didn't, and Alice jumped out from behind the counter and got between him and the door.

"I would like to leave," he said quietly. "I think it's best."

"I don't. And it's my kitchen." Of course Alice would do this. Alice always did this, pushed him and pushed him. She reached out for him and he flinched away. Feeling like he had when he was a teenager, like if she touched him something might break. His skin might slide right off revealing some part of himself he was too scared to see.

She looked up over Cameron's shoulder at Max. And Cameron was sure in that moment he would be unable to look that man in the eye ever again. Which meant, really...

he needed to leave, like...for good. Not just for the night. But he had to get gone.

"Max," Alice said. "Put away your cop brain for a second."

Max shook his head and Alice sighed.

"We know how those two feel about each other. We've known for years. This kind of thing was always going to happen."

"That doesn't make groping her while she's drunk all right!" Max said.

"No," Cameron said in total agreement, and he could try and explain what happened, but the explanation was lame. Because he'd felt himself melting on that bed. And he'd promised to take care of her. He'd failed this family. "It doesn't."

"Max," Alice said. "This is Cameron. Whatever happened...whatever you saw...I think it's safe to say there was more to the story. If there's one thing the Mitchells know it's that there is always more to the story."

Cameron heard the scrape of a stool and Max's heavy breath as he sat, and Alice sighed and gave him a brief quick smile.

"Sit down," Max said. "Tell us what happened."

Cameron didn't sit and he didn't talk because he could see in Max's face that his opinion was set. And Alice kept herself busy putting the nachos he was never going to eat in the oven under the broiler. Delia came down, looking worried and resigned.

Cameron felt his face get hot and red, and he looked away. The guilt squeezed his chest so tight he could barely breathe. Part of him wanted to be mad again. But mad was too easy. Mad was what his father would have done. Mad was what he would have done years ago. Slipping into that skin...so easy. Standing here and trying to explain how he'd made one mistake but truly wasn't going to make another one...impossible.

"I'll tell you what happened," Delia said, kissing her husband's cheek and sighing. "Our daughter got just drunk enough to finally tell Cameron how she feels. She said she kissed him. She said she accidentally pulled him onto the bed."

"Is that true?" Max asked.

"Does it change anything?" Cameron asked. "Does it make my part in it okay?"

"Maybe," Alice said.

"No," Max said.

Delia rolled her eyes and smacked her husband's shoulder. "Stop."

"No." He shook his head. "I won't. Cameron knows what he did was wrong."

"Cameron?" Delia asked. "Do you love Josie?"

"It doesn't matter. Because it doesn't change the fact that I trusted you," Max said to Cameron, and that was really what it came down to. Every bit of it. He'd betrayed Max. Josie. The whole family. "And then I found you on top of her."

"Max..." Delia started to chastise him but Cameron hadn't said a word to anyone about his feelings for Josie. Not until tonight, and it didn't seem right to talk about his feelings with anyone but her, but he couldn't have Max thinking what he felt was...cheap. Or convenient.

"I love her," Cameron said.

"And she's been watching him with her heart in her eyes since she was fifteen," Delia said

Max looked unconvinced. He looked like he was still ready to murder Cameron.

All of a sudden, Cameron remembered being a kid in his father's home. And being too young to understand that what he needed he'd never get, but being scared to leave. It had seemed, even suffering his dad's neglect and abuse, easier to stay and be hated and miserable than it was to leave. So he'd waited too long to leave. He'd wasted years festering in a garbage situation.

"I think...I think it's best if I just leave," Cameron said.

"And go where?" Alice asked. "You live here."

"But maybe I shouldn't anymore. You've been on me for months now about what my plans are for the future."

"Well, this isn't a plan. This is just running away. Max!" Alice cried. "Help me!"

"I don't know," Max said. "Maybe this is for the best."

"What?" Alice and Delia both turned on him, aghast.

"Maybe..." Max shrugged. "Maybe this was the push we all needed to help him figure it out."

"This isn't helping anything," Delia said. "It's kicking Cameron out."

"It's not," Cameron said. "I think...Max is right." He even managed to smile at Max, like they were on the same side. Like the relationship they had wasn't over.

You were the only father I really ever had. He wished he could say that, but his words were shit. He knew that. Max didn't care.

"He's not." Alice shook her head.

"You've been on me for months now. A year, even. To figure out what I was going to do next. I'm doing that." Cameron shrugged, like it was all no big deal.

"No, you're leaving because Max is scaring you and you're upset and freaked out. This is not the time to make that decision."

Max was silent, and even Delia was quiet and he got

that. He'd burned through the trust they had for him. Now he just needed Alice to understand.

"If I stay," Cameron said, feeling that sick ball in his stomach climb up in his throat. *If I stay in the only home I've ever known, with the only people I've ever loved and who ever showed me kindness...* Oh fuck. He couldn't say that. "If I stay tomorrow you'll have a job for me and then another job. You'll do everything you can to make me stay—"

"No, I won't," Alice lied. Smoke was coming out of the oven so he walked over, grabbed the tea towel, and pulled the blackened nachos out of the oven. He set them on the counter and knew in his gut that he would never be able to eat nachos again.

"You will. And I'll let you. And...I would stay and learn everything you can teach me and not once think about learning anything else. Or experiencing anything else. I would have..." He swallowed and shook his head, and it was so hard to say. So hard. "I would have loved Josie and never learned to love anyone else."

"Oh Cameron," Delia whispered.

"I mean, if one thing was proven by tonight it's that..." He looked over at Max. *Please,* he thought, *please give me this. At least give me this.* "I need to grow up a little away from this place. Away from all of you. Away from Josie."

He one hundred percent didn't mean any of this bullshit. But he had to get out of there.

"I'm twenty-two. An adult," he said. "And maybe it's time I acted like it." *Or felt like it.*

And then, suddenly, Max nodded.

Alice sighed.

And the whole vibe in the room changed and...well, it was happening.

Holy shit. I'm leaving.

"Okay," Alice said. "Tomorrow come back here. Gabe and I have saved some money for you over the years. For college or travel. Whatever. It's yours. I can send some letters of recommendation to some colleagues. You could go work for Andreas or Jerome in France."

There. Now Alice was on board.

"Okay," he said. "I'll come back tomorrow and we can figure it out."

He even smiled as he headed for the door. His car. And whatever came next.

"You have to talk to Josie," Delia said. "You can't leave things like this. She'll be devastated."

"Of course," he said. *And say what?* he wondered. *I love you and I ruined everything? I love you and your family wants me to leave?* What good was that going to do? *Go be amazing,* that's what he would say to her. *Go be the writer you dream of being and I'll be all right.*

"Okay," Alice said. It killed him to lie to her. But there wasn't any other way. "Sorry about the nachos," she said.

Tears burned in his eyes and in his throat, and he nodded and waved goodbye and got the fuck out of there. He was halfway to his car before he realized Max had followed him.

"Cameron," he said.

No. Nope. No way. "I'm leaving Max...I'll see you tomorrow."

"We both know that's a lie. I know what leaving looks like."

Cameron stopped. "Don't try to stop me. I know you don't mean it."

"I'm not here to stop you."

The bitter laugh clawed its way out of his throat and broke like a sob.

"Here," Max said. "Take this."

Cameron turned to see Max holding out a wad of money. "I'm not taking that."

"Yeah you are," Max said and just shoved it into Cameron's backpack. "You're gonna need it."

He stared up at the moon, refusing to cry and refusing to look at Max. "You would have stopped," Max said. "I can't let you leave here thinking that you might not have. You are a good man."

"That's not what you were saying before."

"Sometimes it's hard to forget what I've seen," Max said, and it only made Cameron more angry. "She was drunk. About to throw up—"

"And I was on top of her. I get it. I was there."

"Josie—"

Yeah. He wasn't going to stand there and talk about Josie with Max. How she was better off away from him and this place, when all he'd ever wanted was this place and her. He turned and started walking to his car.

"What should I tell her?" Max asked. 'Tomorrow when she wakes up and feels like garbage. What should I tell her?"

I love her. I've always loved her. I will always love her. She deserves the world and everything in it, and if anyone ever dares to hurt her I will personally come and destroy their life.

But one look at Max's face and Cameron understood she already had a person for that. And Cameron was on the other side of it. The other side of everything. He'd let down the family and now he was on the outside in every way.

"Tell her this is for the best."

2
____

2 019

Hey Josie!

Congrats on the new season. *Jonah said you got a promotion...
Head Writer and Executive Producer? (Insert Jonah's joke here
about writers on a reality tv show. Insert my groan.) That's so
amazing. I always knew you were going to be a big deal. I was
sorry I missed you last month. Our trip got all turned around and
Evan and I had to stay in Albany an extra week. Organic
Farming Government Lobbying—who knew it was so dramatic?
Anyway, I know your schedule is just crammed during the holi-
days so I want to get this request in early. Well... not a request.
Christmas wish? Christmas demand? Yeah.*

Demand.

You need to come home to the Riverview for Christmas.

Here are the reasons:

1. *It's Christmas and you haven't been home for Christmas in FIVE YEARS. Even typing that makes me shake my head. I know your job is important, but so is drinking hot cocoa by the fire with ME.*
2. *Everyone misses you. Especially me.*
3. *The wi-fi out there is SOLID so you can still work. Jonah got the whole mountain's internet improved so he could work. So, work is 100% not an excuse.*
4. *I'm pregnant.*

Okay, before you freak out. I'm five months. It was touch and go for the first three and we didn't tell anyone. I wanted to tell you last month in person but work got in the way. And... Josie. I just want to see you. And it's Christmas. And I'm pregnant. Please come home.

Helen

JOSIE

THE RIVERVIEW INN at Christmas was a total show-off. All the white twinkle lights in the snow-dusted pine trees. The windows filled with the warm glow of fireplaces. The gigantic red and gold wreath on the front door. Even nature was contributing to the scene; snow was coming down in big, fat Hollywood flakes, like the whole world was in a snow globe that had just been twirled upside down.

It looked, actually, like every Christmas set Josie had

ever tried to create but somehow failed to. It didn't matter how much money they put into set design or props, it was just never quite right.

It's the smell, she thought. *You just can't recreate the smell of snow and pine trees.* It was so powerful it was practically a taste on the tip of her tongue.

The Uber drove off behind her. Leaving Josie and her bags standing at the entrance of the inn. Feeling an excruciating combination of dread and excitement.

Smile. Keep smiling. Don't stop smiling.

As coping mechanisms went it was fairly lame, but it was all she had and so she was committed. Besides, there was usually enough mayhem in her family that she could blend in and escape too much notice.

Though the five years she'd been gone were going to be a *thing*.

Christmas was a few days away and everyone was home for the holiday. Mom and Dad. Gabe and Alice. Jonah and Daphne, Josie's half-brother Dom and all the cousins. This place was absolutely filled with Mitchells. She could practically hear them arguing about table setting and laughing over Dom's hair.

Why am I scared?

She knew that she shouldn't be. It didn't make sense.

But her heart was pounding in her neck. And her hands were slick in her gloves.

The inn looked somehow bigger and smaller than she remembered. But that was the way of memory, wasn't it? It played tricks like that all the time. Like the emotion attached to things changed the scale of places or the color of walls. Her heart changed the size and shape of the front door and planted trees where there weren't any. It was familiar and completely strange all at the same time.

Five years since she'd been here.

"You can't turn back now," a voice said behind her and she turned to see Patrick wearing a thick coat and big hat making his way up the road toward her.

Smile. Keep smiling.

"I wasn't going to," Josie said with a big smile as the man who'd been the best grandfather she could imagine came to a stop in front of her.

"I'd like to hug you," he said, his eyes twinkling.

"I'd like to hug you too," she said, and the words weren't even out of her mouth before he had his arms around her. He smelled like snow and Old Spice.

Okay. New coping mechanism. Don't cry. Just don't cry.

"We missed you, girl."

"I doubt that," she said.

That made Patrick lurch back and frown at her. His eyebrows were exceptionally white and bushy. And capable of a lot of disapproval. "No," she said, trying to backtrack to avoid a lecture about her spot in the Mitchell family. "I'm just saying there are so many cousins and kids now—"

"None of them are you, kid," he said and gave her a little shake.

"Hardly a kid anymore," Josie said with a smile. Turning twenty-four this year had been strange. She'd felt it more than she'd felt any other birthday. Probably because she'd been alone. By choice, mind you. Mom and Dad usually came down for her birthday, took her shopping and out to dinner. Max always looked surprisingly comfortable in the city. The mountain man persona he cultivated up here just fell away and he was the city cop once again. Pretty handsome in a suit and tie, ordering oysters at restaurants like he'd always done it.

Mom always looked at Max a little differently when they

were in the city. Like he was a stranger she'd just met. Josie did not want to think about what they got up to in the hotel room they always rented.

But this year her birthday had fallen right in the middle of release week for the show and there'd been just too much going on to celebrate.

Or, at least, it had been convenient to say that.

"Dad?" Max yelled from the front step, the door open behind him revealing the long dining room table set for dinner, the fireplace, and about seven hundred of Josie's cousins. The beautiful mayhem of Mitchell life at the Riverview Inn. Her heart gushed a fresh, painful longing.

"What are you doing out here?" Max yelled.

"Look who I found," Patrick shouted back, and like he wasn't a gazillion years old, he picked up her bag, swung it over his shoulder and pretty much pulled her into motion.

"Oh my god," Max said. "Josie?"

He glanced behind him and she knew what he was thinking. *Tell Delia.*

It was one of the reasons she loved Max, because his first thought was always about Mom. It was pure, that kind of love. But then Max jumped down the steps in his socks and grabbed Josie in his big arms. Crushed the breath right out of her.

"My god, girl," he said.

Josie held herself stiff in his arms, because if she wasn't stiff, if she wasn't strong and careful, it would be nothing but tears. This homecoming needed to be happy. For Mom's sake. For Helen's sake.

For hers.

Smile.

"Hi Dad," she whispered against the soft flannel of his

shirt. Red, because Mom always said he looked handsome in red.

"What...why didn't you tell us you were coming tonight? We could have met you at the train. I could have come and—"

So predictable, this guy. "Because work was a question mark until the very last minute and I didn't want to inconvenience anyone."

They'd known she was coming; she'd called with that news the second she'd accepted Helen's demands. But she'd been sketchy on the details, hoping if she caught them all slightly unaware there wouldn't be any production.

She saw all the old gears turning behind Max's eyes, but in typical Max fashion he just nodded, took the bag from his own father and pulled Josie up into the inn.

If she paused at the door, scared and a little haunted, he just held on tighter. Harder. *I got you, kid*, his arm around her shoulder said. *I got you.*

"Hey," he said, and every Mitchell there turned to face them. "Look who I found."

Josie lifted her hand, smiling as hard and as brightly as she could. "Hi!"

There was one second of open-mouthed astonishment. And then it was pandemonium.

Garth and Stella, who was in high school now. Little Iris, who'd been born just before everything fell apart. Her half-brother, Dom, who'd hit puberty hard and had grown five inches in all directions since she saw him last summer in the city. Gabe and Alice and Jonah and Daphne. Hugs and kisses and *oh-my-god-look-at-you*s. Stella asked if she could borrow Josie's boots—heeled Pradas that had no business out in this snow.

"Sure," she said with a big smile.

Helen appeared in front of her, looking beautiful in leggings and a bright red sweater pulled taut over her tiny belly. Her cousin was showing off and Josie loved it.

"You came," Helen said, squeezing Josie's cheeks

"You told me I had to," Josie answered awkwardly. "You really are pregnant."

Helen, her cousin and her oldest and dearest friend, smiled, tears in her eyes. "I really am."

And then it was Mom's turn, cutting through all of them, pushing aside everyone to get to Josie. And Josie slipped right out of the numbness she'd been trying to keep around herself and grabbed onto her mother just as hard as Delia grabbed onto Josie.

The sound that came out of Josie was a sob, but as quick as she could, she turned it into a laugh.

Mom squeezed Josie tighter like she knew.

"Welcome home," Mom whispered. "We missed you."

"I missed you, too."

But her mom, who really was rarely wrong, was wrong about one thing.

This wasn't her home anymore. And it hadn't been since the night of her high school graduation.

3

———

"So," Jonah said, leaning back from the table, his hand on Daphne's shoulder. Alice's dinner, a feast of pasta carbonara and salad with blood oranges and pistachios, was absolutely decimated. The dishes in the middle of the table were empty. The plates in front of everyone practically licked clean. Josie had missed the food at the inn with an acute ache. Because of Alice, and in turn Cameron, she'd never learned a thing about cooking; the best she could do for herself was takeout. She even screwed up hard-boiled eggs.

"How is work, Josie?" Jonah asked. And of course Jonah asked; the guy had enough work ethic for, like, twenty people. He'd been a big-deal developer in the city before he met Daphne and gave it all up to grow vegetables on her organic farm and start Haven House—his dream project for single moms and their kids. Growing up with a single Mom Jonah had dreamt of a place where his mother could not just relax but get instruction on things that she never had time to learn. And that dream had turned into a reality with women and kids getting educations, counseling and therapy, second chances. It was all really beautiful, but the guy was nonstop, no matter what he did. His idea of a vacation was a 10K run.

"Fine," she said. "Good. Busy." Jonah had helped her get the job when she was still at NYU by putting her in touch with an executive at the NOW network. Her résumé and his recommendation had circled around the network until she'd landed an internship at the reality show *I Do/I Don't.*

An internship that had turned into a job.

"How is the promotion?" he asked.

"Good." And cue Jonah...

"I can't believe a reality show has a head writer."

Cue family groans.

"You gotta stop the Dad jokes, Uncle Jonah," Dom said in his ever-bored teenage boy voice.

"Can't stop. Won't stop," Jonah shot back, and Dom rolled his eyes.

Josie's brother had changed his hair. He'd been growing out the front in that Justin Beiber-esque flop that had ruled the world for a while. Now he seemed to have...a mullet?

Josie had so many questions.

"I cannot believe Adriane left Hank at the altar," Stella, Josie's cousin, was a die-hard fan of the show and was always up for gossip. "Did you know that was going to happen?"

"Producers had a pretty good idea," Josie said.

She couldn't spill all the secrets about her job as a writer at the reality TV show, even to her family. She'd signed a very scary contract that laid out just how much trouble she could be in if she did. And as executive producer she'd fired interns and assistants and some cast members for tweeting and snap-chatting and talking to TMZ. But once someone found out she worked on *I Do/I Don't*, that's all they wanted to talk about.

"But I really liked Jill and Sam," Stella said.

"I did too," Josie admitted. They'd agreed to pretend to be in a relationship to extend the social media glow they were both enjoying. It was about as contrived and business-focused as a show about love could be.

But they were decent people and total professionals.

Josie wanted to tell Stella what she was planning for the show. The pitch she'd created that the rest of the team was reviewing. Shifting the show from a contrived dating show to...a social experiment. Her plan was to bring people in from different walks of life, different races, religions, sexual orientations, and gender identifications, and instead of falling in love and forcing marriage, they'd talk to each other. Learn who the others were behind the differences that, in today's world, seemed all-important. And create real communication and show *real examples* of how—at the heart of everything—humans were so much more alike than anyone thought.

Josie thought it could be groundbreaking. She believed it was groundbreaking. But her bosses were discussing it now, and even though things looked good for her plan, nothing was ever set in stone. But she had an excited energy in her stomach that told her this was going to happen. The show was going to be something they could all be proud of.

"Hey," Dom said. "I saw that picture of you in *People* magazine."

"Let's not get carried away. You saw the picture of the side of my face," she said. Ben, a stockbroker who'd been after her for a date, had finally caught her with tickets to a hot new Broadway musical. He'd spent the night trying to get their picture taken. It had been more than a little gross.

But she'd met Lin-Manuel Miranda, so the night hadn't been a total waste.

But that picture came out with her name in the caption and her family acted like she'd met the queen. It was adorkable.

"You're so famous," Mom teased.

Josie rolled her eyes.

"But honey," Mom said. Her red hair had a little bit more gray in it than the last time Josie had seen her in the summer, but she was still a total knockout. Josie had her birth father's height, but the rest of her was a carbon copy of her mother. She was grateful on all fronts. "Last year you were looking for a new job..."

This again. And at Christmas? Come on, Mom.

Last year one of the male contestants had said some really offensive things on Twitter and it had been the last straw for a lot of staff. There'd been a serious exodus of production people. She'd made the mistake of telling her mom that she was *thinking* about looking for a new job.

But honest to god, she'd just been too busy. Still was. Right now she could feel her phone in her back pocket buzzing with about seven thousand notifications from her messenger and email.

And her bosses had that sixth sense about anyone thinking of looking for another job, and they'd set the trap of a promotion and salary bump like putting out Christmas cookies for Santa Claus.

And everyone had fallen for it. She'd thought she'd be different.

She hadn't been.

And then she got this new idea and this new energy. She just couldn't tell her mom about it, yet. Not until it was a done deal.

"Why am I getting all the questions?" Josie laughed, setting her fork down next to the pear tarte Alice had made for dessert. "Am I the only one who has a million questions for Helen?"

"Yeah, yeah, she's pregnant," Daphne said, winking at her daughter. "Big deal."

Helen smiled her cypher's smile and ran a hand over her stomach.

"How long has everyone known?" Josie asked.

"Mom says she woke up in the middle of the night five months ago and knew something was different," Helen said.

"I've always said you two were a little too close," Alice said from her place at the end of the table, next to Gabe. And Stella, her daughter and only child, laughed.

"Mom," the teenager cried. "You still ask if you can sleep with me."

"I just like your bed better."

It was a lie and everyone knew it. Even Gabe, who gave her a comforting pat on the shoulder. On the other side of the table, Josie had a hard time looking at Gabe and Alice, and chose instead to focus on Helen. Blonde and pregnant and looking so happy it was like she'd swallowed a lightbulb.

"You really are glowing," Josie said.

"I really am happy."

"Where's Evan?" Josie asked. Helen's longtime boyfriend and the father of the lightbulb.

"He's still in DC," Helen said. "He should be here on Christmas Eve."

"Isn't that cutting it close?" Josie asked. Because while Christmas as a whole was a big deal at the Riverview, the real star of the show was Christmas Eve. The outrageous number of traditions that had been piled onto Christmas

Eve was nearly insane. No holiday should have to be so much to a single family. But the Mitchells were not like other families.

And Christmas Eve was only three days away.

"That's the plan," Helen said. Evan and Helen both worked for a nonprofit organic farmers' association that lobbied state and federal government to try and change laws and regulations.

They were two very adorable do-gooders.

"And seriously..." Josie lowered her voice. "You're not getting any flack about not being married."

"Are you kidding me? With this crowd?" Helen looked around their assembled family. Gabe and Alice, who'd been married before and had three horrible miscarriages that had ultimately ended their relationship the first time around. But when Gabe opened the inn and needed a chef, he'd begged Alice to come and work with him. Of course they hadn't been able to keep their hands off each other, and when she'd ended up pregnant she tried to keep it a secret.

Gabe insisted they get married but they didn't actually do it until *after* Stella had been born.

Iris, their grandmother, sitting across the table with Patrick, had left her two sons in a terrible bout of post-partum depression only to find out she was pregnant again. She'd asked to come back but Patrick had said no, so she'd kept Jonah a secret from the rest of the family for years.

It hadn't been pretty when they first got back together, but it was now. Proof, maybe, that things always got better, even when they were really dark.

"Yeah, the Mitchells don't exactly do things in order," Josie said with a smile, feeling that gush of affection she had for her unorthodox family.

"Well..." Alice, at the head of the table, sighed. "I made this meal. I'm sure as hell not cleaning it up."

"I got it." Josie jumped to her feet and began clearing dishes. Wanting so badly to be useful and busy, and away from everyone's curiosity about her life. And—she was adult enough to admit it—wanting somehow to change the way Alice looked at her.

Everyone told her in quiet voices that Alice didn't blame her for Cameron leaving. But the way Alice looked at her said otherwise.

Not that dishes would do it—but it felt like a start.

The kitchen of the Riverview was the unofficial heart of the place and it had grown over the years, just as the inn had grown. Gabe used to have an office next to it, but the walls had been taken down to make room for a bigger industrial oven and dishwasher. The windows in the far corner revealed the jet-black night and the tiny pinpricks of stars over the mountains. Josie set the plates down on the stainless steel table where she'd tried and failed to learn how to bake. It was where she'd helped plan the area school lunches. It's where she and Helen had eaten a million pieces of cold pizza and giggled about boys.

It's where she'd fallen in love.

And had her heart broken.

Where is he? she'd asked the morning after her graduation. Sick to her stomach and shaky, and so humiliated her bones hurt. She couldn't see straight. Alice had given her coffee, but it made everything worse.

He's gone, Max had said.

Where?

We don't know, Alice had snapped. Her eyes were red, too, and she was pissed. At Josie and Max.

Did you make him leave? she'd asked Max. *Because of me?*

No, Max had said. *He...he left on his own.*

Alice had made a noise in her throat and turned away, and Josie had bent over her legs but that hadn't made anything better so she'd run to the back door and barely made it out onto the gravel before throwing up.

It's not what you think, Max had said when he came out with a glass of water and a towel. He was sad, too. Everyone had been so fucking sad because she'd made some kind of horrible fool of herself and sexually assaulted her best friend.

Oh, she'd said sarcastically. *That makes me feel better.*

Honestly. Max had tried to put his arm around her, but she'd shrugged her whole body away, unable—absolutely unable maybe ever, ever again—to be touched. *This is for the best, Josie. That's what he said.*

She'd blinked back the thick tears and looked at Max. He'd looked old in the sunshine. Tired.

He said that? she'd asked. She hadn't remembered a bunch of the previous night—things were fuzzy, at best— but she remembered he'd kissed her back. He'd kissed her back like she mattered. Like she'd dreamed of being kissed for years. She couldn't remember what they said to each other, but that was crystal clear.

But that had been just sex, maybe. That had just been a drunk girl throwing herself at a guy. And him catching her for a second before putting her aside.

He never loved me.

He never wanted me.

The previous day she would have sworn on her life that she and Cameron were soul mates.

She'd been disastrously wrong.

That's what he said, Max had told her. *It's for the best.*

Shaking off the memories she turned toward the second

big fridge where the family kept their food. The fridge on the other side of the room was for the inn. Alice always said it was a bookkeeping thing, but everyone knew it was so no one ate her favorite cheese and the olives she liked, or the green apples she had every morning with her breakfast.

The kitchen was dark; the only light was from the moon and the lights in the dining room coming in through the open door, so it took Josie a second to realize what she was looking at on the front of the fridge.

Postcards. A dozen of them, at least.

Spain. Portugal. France. Nepal. Morocco.

And she knew without looking at them who they were from and who they were to. And it felt like an invasion of privacy to read them, but she couldn't help herself. They were there. Right there on the fridge. They were meant to be read.

She picked up Greetings from Morocco and flipped it over.

Figs, Alice! Fresh yogurt from goats. Runny honey and black pepper. Breakfast of champs. Put it on the menu. Love Cameron

This was the closest she'd been to him since that night. Reading his name on a postcard.

Her heart pounded so hard, her whole body shook.

And she wanted to press her face to the card—to his handwriting—like a crazy woman. Like his smell might still be there. Like somehow she could feel him from so far and so many years away.

Fingers trembling, she put it back.

These messages weren't for her; she knew that. It was an invasion of privacy. And salt in the wounds she'd caused everyone that night.

She picked up another one. Sweden.

There were two recipes on the back. One for cinnamon

rolls with cloves and cardamom and the other for brined salmon.

I miss you was scrawled across the bottom.

Cameron had terrible handwriting. He always had. The notes he used to leave for her had been unreadable but she'd deciphered them like learning a foreign language. And being able to read his handwriting had felt like something special, like she'd cracked the code of him. Ridiculous, but when you're a teenager and nursing unrequited love, you'll cobble together a case for just about anything.

She replaced the card on the fridge and stepped back. There were twenty cards on the front and another thirty on the side.

London. Tokyo. Auckland. Beijing. Sao Paulo.

Each of them a recipe. Each of them a love letter from around the world to the woman who'd been a mother to him.

The woman he'd left behind.

Because of Josie. Because she'd been so stupid and pushed an issue that shouldn't have been pushed and rather than jeopardize the family—he'd left.

The guilt that she'd managed by being far away and keeping herself busy and—if she was really being honest—shoving the memories as deep as they could go, now resurfaced and was heavier than it had ever been. Her knees buckled and she put her hand against the fridge, her pinky resting against a sheep's nose on a postcard from New Zealand.

Cameron. I'm so sorry.

"Josie?"

Of course it was Alice behind her. Josie closed her eyes in grim defeat. The one person she simply couldn't talk to right now.

This moment had been coming. She'd known it the second she read that email from Helen. It was the reason she'd had a heartbeat of hesitation before she said yes.

They had to talk, she and Alice.

She just couldn't do it now. Not yet.

There were other people coming into the kitchen behind Alice. Josie heard Stella and Grandma Iris—but Alice told them to wait just a minute in the dining room.

Do this. You can do this. And smile!

Josie turned, her expression more a grimace than a smile, but she gave herself points for trying. Even though she knew the smile did not hide the tears standing in her eyes and the guilt she carried and the love she didn't ever know what to do with in the absence of the person she most wanted to lavish it upon.

"Are you all right?" Alice asked. Alice wasn't cold. To think she was cold was a pretty classic misconception about her. She was fierce and she was serious. And she did not throw her heart around easily. But once you were hers, you were hers.

Josie had just never been hers. Not the way Cameron had been.

Alice looked like that actress Winona Ryder, only perpetually caught in the nineties version of her. No one kept pixie haircuts, denim shirts, and Doc Martens alive quite like Alice. It was one of the more endearing things about her. She did not change.

It was also one of the more terrifying things about her.

And the morning after Josie's birthday, Alice had said everything that happened wasn't Josie's fault.

But she'd been lying.

"I'm so sorry." Josie had said it before and saying it again, so many years later, seemed ridiculous, but she didn't know what else to say.

Alice looked out the window, her pale skin gleaming in the moonlight. She swallowed and swallowed again, but when she turned to Josie she was smiling.

But the smile was a lie. Just like Josie's smile. One of the two things they had in common.

"We should talk," Alice said.

And Josie knew that was true. Part of her even wanted it. Closure all these years after the fact.

"Okay," Josie said. "But not now."

"No," Alice agreed like she was happy for the respite. "Later."

"Can I ask...?"

"What?"

"Is he all right?"

"Cameron?"

Oh. No one had said that name aloud in years. Not to her. "Yeah."

"You haven't...talked to him?"

Josie shook her head.

"Lately?" Alice asked.

I haven't talked to him since that night. Seven years. I told him I loved him. I kissed him. He left.

"No," she said. And that he hadn't answered her texts or emails or reached out with his own, more than his leaving, told her everything she needed to know about his feelings for her.

Alice blinked like Josie had stunned her.

"Have you seen Five Questions?" Alice finally asked.

Five Questions was Cameron's hybrid cooking/travel YouTube channel that had started four years ago in the most Cameron type way—he'd ask five questions every morning while making coffee no matter where he was or what he had available. Coffee on the sides of mountains, in remote villages, using that camping coffee maker she'd given him for his birthday. (The sight of that little thing had been like a knife to her heart.) Some days he asked strangers. Some days he asked himself, if no one was around. And if it had started bare-bones, in the last few years there'd been moments of poshness. He'd made coffee in a suite at the Ritz in Paris. In the kitchens of Buckingham Palace. At Jimmy Fallon's home in The Hamptons. And it wasn't just coffee anymore. He'd started making food from ancient recipes. Gnocchi from someone's nonna in Sicily. Goat cheese from herders in Peru.

But always Five Questions. For himself. For his viewers. And his guests.

Originally, it had been strangers. Some days just himself. But for the last year he'd been pulling real guests.

Famous chefs. Not just the ones on The Food Network. But Michelin starred chefs. All out there learning something fundamental about their craft, or something luxurious or quirky. Answering five sometimes ridiculous, sometimes intrusive questions. The episode with Jose Andreas in Spain catching fish—when Cameron got seasick and Jose fell into the water—went viral.

Cameron and their old game and the coffeemaker she'd given him for this birthday were all something of a phenomenon.

Not that she stalked him on his YouTube channel. Except when she'd had too much to drink.

And on her birthday. And last Wednesday.

"I've seen it," Josie said.

Alice smiled her razor's edge smile, like she understood Josie downplaying it all.

"He's good. He travels a lot. He was engaged for about a minute."

Josie sucked in a breath. That shouldn't hurt. *Why did it hurt?*

"But they never got married."

"I'm sorry to hear that."

"He says it was for the best."

It's for the best. The four worst words in any language.

"He's the same old Cameron, you know," Alice said. "Stubborn. Creative. Works hard. But he's different too. Relaxed a little. Like he doesn't have to prove himself all the time."

There was something laced in those words. A kind of benediction. Like she was telling Josie that Cameron's leaving really had been for the best. Or, if not the best, had at least had a bright side.

"He stopped asking after you about a year after he left," Alice said, stepping closer and then stopping, like she felt the force field Josie had up. "I thought maybe he got in touch with you."

"No." Josie managed a smile. "He just..." *Forgot about me?* "Moved on. Which, you know, is good."

"Have *you*?" Alice asked, which frankly seemed like the dumbest question ever. Josie was standing in a dark kitchen in tears over some postcards that had nothing to do with her.

"Of course," she said, and it wasn't totally a lie.

Josie was saved from any more conversation by Grandma Iris walking in the door bearing an empty serving tray. Alice rushed to take it from Iris's shaking hands. The cousins followed carrying dirty dishes. "Josie!" Stella said. "Do you think I could apply for that summer internship program at your network this year?"

"You need to be in college," Josie said.

"Yeah, but aren't there some strings you can pull?" Stella waggled her eyebrows and Josie shook her head, and as promised, the mayhem of the Mitchell family took the pressure off her and within a few minutes she found herself escaping the kitchen.

And the postcards.

It was too bad the boy who wrote them was not so easy to escape.

"I can't believe you're here," Helen said, an hour later as she and Josie sat in the quiet of the lodge. Helen, holding her hand to her stomach, shifted and then shifted again, struggling to get comfortable on the leather couch in front of the fireplace that was, as a rule, the most comfortable piece of furniture ever made. Only pregnancy could make it uncomfortable. And Josie, sitting next to her on the same couch was getting tossed around like they were at sea by all of Helen's shifting.

"Helen." Josie laughed. "You made it very clear that if I wasn't here this year for Christmas you were going to disown me."

"I didn't say that!" Helen cried.

"I read between the lines."

"Well...enough is enough and all that. You should be here for Christmas, and if you didn't come, you'd never see what a cute pregnant lady I am."

"You are a very cute pregnant lady."

"Right?" Helen asked, preening a little. And the girl had the right to preen.

"So, you and Evan?" Josie asked. "I guess it's for real now."

Helen smiled. She and Evan had always been for real, from the second they met at university in Boston. Peas and Carrots, Grandma Iris had called them. Which was the highest compliment a couple could be given in Iris speak.

"I can't believe you haven't been back to the Riverview in five years."

"Me neither, really," Josie said.

"What do you do at Christmas?"

"Work."

"You're joking."

"Nope. I have to work while I'm here. We're casting for the new season. It's actually a really busy time of year." They were still creating a new season of *I Do/I Don't* and hopefully transitioning to her new idea next year.

"You really are a big deal," Helen said, nudging Josie's shoulder and grinning. "Hotshot."

"Hardly."

"You must make a shit ton of money."

"Are you going to ask for another donation?" Josie pretended to tease. Donating to Helen's cause was literally the least she could do.

"No. But..." Helen sighed. "I love my job and I believe in it, but with the kid coming I think either Evan or I need to get something that earns a little more or is a little bit more stable."

"You know the family will support you."

Helen nodded, but stared off into the flames, her hand over her stomach. That was the funny thing about a family like the Mitchells. They could make it real comfortable to rely on them.

To stay, even. To be a part of the legacy here rather than step outside and find something of your own.

It was tricky.

"It must be weird being here without Cameron," Helen said.

Again that name. It hit like a smack and Josie couldn't stop the flinch.

"Please," she whispered. Helen was the only person she could admit this to, and even that felt like too much. "Don't. I can do this, I can be here and I can even be happy, but if we talk about him..." She couldn't actually finish the sentence. Living with a mistake like the one she'd made required extreme compartmentalization. She had it squished down into a box, but the box was leaking and making a mess, and she was compensating for that box in a lot of different parts of her life, but it was closed.

And it was never—ever—opened.

"I need...to tell you something," Helen said. Her tone was serious and Josie put a hand on Helen's shoulder. They were cousins by marriage, but truly sisters at heart.

"What? Is everything all right?" Josie asked, alarmed by Helen's sudden seriousness.

"Fine, but...I don't want you to be surprised—"

"Hey girls." It was Max, coming in from outside. A bitter December-in-the-Catskills wind blew in around him, making the flames in the fireplace dance and sputter. Snow dusted his hair and shoulders. "Snow's coming down. You gonna bunk in the lodge tonight?"

"Slumber party?" Josie asked, wiggling her eyebrows. Max and Mom had built a cabin on the far side of the property, but for Josie, home was always going to be the bedroom she'd shared with her mother when they first moved here. The room she got to herself when Mom moved into Max's room.

Helen sighed. "I can't. I promised Mom we'd do some shopping in the morning. I need to head to the farm."

She struggled to get to her feet and Josie stood up to help her.

"Oh my god, I'm a whale," Helen joked.

"You are five months, Helen. And barely showing. You better start pacing yourself."

Helen gasped in mock outrage.

Josie wrapped her arms around her. "Thanks for making me come home," she whispered in Helen's ear. "I'm glad I came."

"So are we," Helen said.

And Josie told herself not to say it, not to bring it up because it was pulling at the lid on that box she liked to pretend didn't exist. But in this lodge, in this home that Alice and Gabe built for all of them, it was hard not to say it. It was the elephant in the room. "I don't think Alice is happy I'm here."

"Of course she is," Helen whispered.

Yeah, it really didn't feel like it.

"Come on girls," Max said and then grinned. "Wow. Serious déjà vu."

Josie smiled at the man who had become the kind of father any girl would be lucky to have. He'd picked up and dropped off Josie and Helen from dances and band practice and dates and school seven million times over the course of their teenage years. Never complaining. Always tuning the radio to their station. Often stopping for contraband McDonald's on the way home.

"I'll give you a ride, Helen," Max said and then smiled, that flickery half smile of his, at Josie. "You, Dom, and I are going tree chopping tomorrow so you need to get some sleep."

Josie looked around the giant dining room and realized there wasn't a tree. It was four days before Christmas and there wasn't a fresh pine tree brushing the ceiling and covered with lights and ornaments.

"Were you waiting—?"

"For you?" Max said. "Of course." At the door Helen was shoving her feet into her boots and wrapping a scarf around her neck. "You gonna stay here for old times' sake or do you want to come back with us?"

"I'm coming," Josie said and put out the fire the way Max taught her and turned off the Christmas lights on the mantel. She blew out the candles on the table and then stepped to the door to put on her stuff and grab her bag.

"That's my girl," Max said and kissed her forehead. And she wished, with a longing she hadn't had in a long time, that the night of her high school graduation hadn't happened and they could be the family they were supposed to be.

4

The cabin that Max had built for his family—Delia, Josie, and then Dom—was on the back corner of the property. Walking between the main lodge and the cabin took about ten minutes, and the drive took about fifteen. Which was just the kind of logic the Riverview was known for.

Mom was legendarily a morning person. And Max had built the whole house to serve that. The kitchen and small breakfast area were wall-to-wall windows and faced the sunrise. There were comfy chairs and a professional coffee machine and even a place for Delia to put out her yoga mat so she could actually salute the sun.

Sitting in this kitchen felt like sitting in her mother's soul in so many ways.

Work, however, was not letting her enjoy it. Josie had been up since five, answering emails and putting out fires. And the "solid Wi-Fi" that Helen had promised to convince her to come home had been a lie.

It was sporadic, at best. She was using her phone as a

hot spot but that wasn't a solution that was going to last this whole week.

She and the team were deep into casting for next season of *I Do/I Don't* and Belinda, the casting director, was forwarding her headshots.

This guy looks like an excellent asshole, what do you think? Belinda texted.

The asshole character was one they had to have every year. People *loved* jerky, privileged muscle-bound men with their Yankees hats on backward.

And this guy was even wearing pookah-shell necklace.

It was enough to make her doubt humanity.

Maybe, Belinda the casting director wrote, *we should have nothing but assholes this season.*

Josie's soul crumpled.

Counterpoint, Josie wrote back. *We do a nothing but nice guys season.*

You know, Belinda wrote, *I can never tell when you're joking.*

Josie ran through the girls' headshots and résumés. Lots of social media influencers and marketers, which was always good for ratings and the long-term health of the series. She checked off three she liked. And then she picked an emergency-room nurse who looked like she might chew up and spit out the backward-hat-wearing dude-bros.

And then, because she could never help herself, a male chef. Because caregiving and competency were always a crowd favorite.

Yeah. That's why she picked the male chefs.

Hey, she texted Belinda. *Has anyone been talking about the pitch I sent Joe and Maryanne last week?*

Yeah. Belinda wrote back.

Josie's heart sputtered. *And?*

So far just water cooler talk. It's a good idea.

"Right?" she said out loud. To her phone. But there was still a season of *I Do/I Don't* to create and work was work.

Looking at the pictures and the backgrounds she wrote up a few loose story notes, ideas about where relationships could go. Yes, it was a reality TV show, and most of the story work happened in editing, but you couldn't leave everything up to chance. You know what happened when you left everything up to chance? Geraldo Rivera and Al Capone's tomb.

"Wow, look at the early bird," Mom said, coming into the kitchen in her pajamas and one of Max's old sweaters. Josie quickly shut her laptop and turned her phone over on the table between the two comfy chairs facing the view. It felt like she was hiding something, and maybe she was. Mom was not an *I Do/I Don't* fan and Josie didn't want to get her mother's hopes up by telling her about the new idea. "How'd you sleep?"

"Fine," Josie lied with a smile. It was so quiet out here in the country, she missed the police sirens and the subway noise and the drunk who yelled on her corner at midnight every night.

The snow-blanketed countryside was so quiet it was loud.

"I'm so glad you're home, honey," Mom said and kissed the top of her head before walking over to the coffeepot.

Josie's phone binged again. And then again.

"Who are you talking to so early in the morning?" Mom asked as she filled up her coffee cup and headed back over to the chairs.

"It's just work," Josie said.

"Just work?"

"Oh Mom, you can't read into everything I say." Josie laughed.

"Well, I'm just reflecting your energy back to you."

"Of course you are, Mom," Josie said with a grin. There were two cosy chairs set up facing the windows with their view of the Catskills and the main lodge, and Mom sat down in the other one.

"Wow, it really snowed last night," Mom said. "We're supposed to get more this week."

"A white Christmas," Josie said.

"Oh my gosh—remember that first Christmas we were here?" Mom asked. "We were so excited about that snow."

"For, like, two seconds, until we realized our Texas winter coats were not going to cut it up here."

"I think my toes were numb for months."

They sipped their coffee and Mom sighed, closing her eyes and letting the sunlight warm her face.

Josie watched her and felt such tenderness for her mom. Such pride that she was this woman's daughter. A survivor. Fierce and brave. "I'm so glad you found this place," Josie said. "The Riverview."

"What a long shot that was, huh?" Mom said with a laugh.

That, when Josie thought about it, was kind of how fate worked. It worked in small ways, sure, but every once in a while, you got this huge flyer. This absolute odds-breaker. And the Riverview and Max were that for Mom. And to some extent for herself—Josie knew that.

"Do you ever think about what would have happened if we didn't end up here?" Josie asked.

"Only in nightmares," Mom whispered. Josie's birth father had been a dirty cop, and after getting full custody of Josie, had tried to kill Mom. It was like something out of a movie. And honestly, if it hadn't happened to them, she wouldn't have believed the story. Mom had escaped and taken Josie with her. They'd hopscotched all over the place before landing here. Where Mom didn't explain to Josie what was going on, and also didn't tell the Mitchells what might be following her.

It took Josie a while to forgive her mom for keeping the secret of the kind of man her father really was and why they were running. But she got it now. Mom had been trying to preserve something for Josie—innocence.

And maybe she just hadn't known how to talk about it.

If there was one thing Josie understood as an adult, it was that it was hard to talk about the hard things. Easier to leave those things alone and hope that everyone could live their lives around the ache and the pain. Like a bruise you just didn't poke, but also a bruise that never healed.

Yeah. She got that.

In the end Max found out what Delia was hiding and managed to keep all of them safe, but not before wounding Josie's birth father in a shoot-out right in the middle of the lodge.

Max and Delia fell in love in the middle of all that drama, and when the time came for Mom to pick a place to settle, her heart made the decision. And the Riverview became their home.

"Are you still loving life in the city?" Mom asked, changing the subject.

"It's exciting," Josie said, which was her pat answer. And it was true—there was always something going on. What she didn't say was that she was too busy to enjoy any of it.

"You know...you can tell me if it's not."

Josie scowled. "Mom, I don't know why you want me to be unhappy."

Delia scowled right back. "There's a difference between wanting you to be unhappy and wanting you to *admit* you're unhappy."

"That's a pretty fine hair you're splitting." Josie took a sip of her coffee in an effort to drown this weird rage in her stomach. *This*, she thought, *this is why I don't come back to the Riverview*. And usually she let it all go—that bruise she never poked. But this morning, exhausted and busy, she felt like poking it.

She put her cup down.

"Is it that you don't like the show? Or that you can't be proud of me because you don't like it?" Josie asked. "I'm the youngest executive producer at the network."

She didn't say anything about how the network chewed up producers like they were gum and somehow—through the sheer stubbornness she'd inherited from her mother, perhaps—she had been the last one standing.

"That's not it. I just feel like you punish yourself with your job. With a job you don't really even like."

Oh, that hit her weird. Like, in her belly. Was that true? It felt true in a way.

"Well, I just feel like all the stuff I've accomplished isn't the right stuff for you," she said. "Like you'd be more proud of me—"

"Stop. Right there. I am proud. So proud." Mom put her hand over Josie's. "I've messed this up. Honey..." She took a deep breath. "I only want you to be happy."

"I'm happy."

A smile teased Mom's lips and Josie understood why. Nothing about the way she'd said those words was convincing. But Josie refused to smile and Mom's smile slowly vanished. And they went back to sipping coffee and looking out over mountains.

"Can I say one more thing?" Delia asked.

"Can I stop you?" Now she was smiling. God. Mom did not change. The phrase *dog with a bone* came to mind.

"You're too good for that show. Too talented. You have big, beautiful ideas and a big, beautiful brain and heart, and you always have."

"That's a nice vote of confidence, Mom, but there are a thousand of me in the city."

"Never," Mom said fiercely and grabbed Josie's hand to kiss it. "Never."

Oh, in staying away from the Riverview she'd also been staying away from her mom, which was a little like starving herself of faith and affection. No one believed in her like her mother, and that kind of power source was sadly lacking in her Queens apartment.

Everyone's mom thought they were extraordinary and she'd gotten used to not having the pressure of living up to that.

"I remember when Max and I dropped you at NYU, and it was like watching your whole life just expand right in front of our eyes. I was so excited for you. You have always been meant for more than the Riverview."

Josie remembered that day, too. The way the three of them had looked at each other with such awareness and excitement. All of them on the edge of *a moment.*

"I always appreciated how you didn't cry," Josie said.

"Cried like a baby when we got in the car."

"I figured." The secret about the show was on the tip of her tongue. And she realized Mom would be happy for her whether her idea was made real or not. She'd be proud of Josie for trying. For pushing for more. So, what was the harm in telling Mom? It would only make Mom happy. An early Christmas present. "Mom?"

Max came out of the long hallway leading to the bedrooms and stopped. "Well, that's a sight," he said, putting his hands on his hips.

"No crying, Max," Mom said. She rolled her eyes at Josie and got up to kiss Max like they hadn't seen each other in days.

Josie looked back out the window. *Tomorrow. I'll tell her tomorrow*, she thought, listening to them whisper to each other the way they always did.

How'd you sleep?

Good. You?

Weird dream about foxes all over the property. They kept trying to get in the house.

That is weird. Freudian.

You think everything is Freudian.

Coffee?

Please.

All she'd ever wanted was what Max and Delia had. Gabe and Alice, Daphne and Jonah. Even Grandma and Grandpa.

A purposeful life.

And a love that could survive everything that got thrown at it.

The great curveball that fate had thrown her way was that she really believed she'd met that person when she was just a kid.

An hour later Max, Dom, and Josie were headed out into the woods to find a Christmas tree. Mom had loaned Josie some boots and a thick winter coat after determining that what Josie had brought from the city was not enough. She was grateful for the boots. And the coat was one of those long ones that went down to her ankles like a giant sleeping bag.

"We need two trees," Max said.

"For what?" Dom asked. He was in the back seat, hood up, head against door, eyes closed. He'd woken up about ten minutes ago and looked like he could go right back to sleep. God. To be a teenager again. Josie was lucky if she got five good hours a night.

"Well, son," Max said, glancing in the rearview mirror as they bounced over the uneven dirt road. "Not sure if you noticed, but we don't have a tree up in our place, either."

"We don't?" Dom asked, cracking one eye.

Max and Josie shared a laughing look. Dom was fourteen, and unless it was food or hockey related, he didn't seem to notice it.

"How's school?" Josie asked her brother, reaching back to shake his knee.

"Fine." He shifted out of the way. "How is New York City?"

"Amazing. You should come visit me."

Dom opened one eye again. "For real?"

"For real," Josie said. Dom could use a little New York in his life. And it had been a very long time since she'd spent any time with him, one on one. The perils of being born so many years apart. They were like strangers who looked alike.

"Hold on," Max said. "The two of you running around New York City unchaperoned—"

"Max, I'm twenty-four."

"And I'm fourteen."

"You're not helping, Dom." Josie laughed at her brother, who grinned at her.

"I'd love to come. We could see a Rangers game."

"Well, I was thinking maybe a Broadway show. Go to some museums."

"And then a Rangers game. And a hot dog. From a cart."

"Oh my god, Alice would die," Josie said. They bounced down a gravel road covered with snow, heading deeper into the forest. Boughs of pine trees slapped against the sides of the truck.

"What we eat in New York, stays in New York," Dom said.

"Particularly if it's street meat," Max said.

"How is hockey?" Josie asked, having put off the only question that really mattered in her brother's life.

He perked right up, and for the next ten minutes Josie got a rundown on hockey stuff she barely understood—but looking at her brother's happy, smiling face was more than enough information.

"Okay, okay," she said. "We'll go to a Rangers game."

"I want to come too," Max said.

"You're not invited."

He pretended to be aghast. But she knew he was thrilled. He and Mom worried about the two of them being born so far apart and never being able to figure out their common ground.

"How is the city treating you?" Max asked.

She laughed. "Like it doesn't know I'm there? How is a city supposed to treat me?"

He glanced over, his eyes smiling. "Just making sure you still like it."

What she liked about it she didn't get to experience much anymore. When she was younger there had always been something new to see. Something completely different. Fun. Neighborhoods and markets. Book readings and Off-Off-Broadway plays. Museums. She even used to do those walking tours, visiting historic crime scenes. Or those food tours through Chinatown. She'd jumped into all of it.

"I'm just really busy," she said, looking out the window. Max let it go.

Finally, they stopped, surrounded by snow and pine trees. The sky was slate gray above them. The trees so green they were nearly black. "All right," he said. "We need a ten-footer for the lodge and a smaller one for our house. I've got—"

"That one and that one," Dom said, pointing out two different trees, one on each side of the truck.

"You think that's ten feet?' Max asked, looking out the window.

"Measure it, but it's ten feet." Dom got out of the truck.

Josie looked at Max who could only shrug. "It's weird, and I don't know how we can make money on it, but he's always right about this stuff."

"It's too bad you can't sell him to the carnival." Josie said.

"You might be on to something. The incredible sleeping, measuring, eating teenage boy."

"Come see him with your own eyes as he guesses how tall you are and then eats your weight in peanut butter sandwiches."

"I can hear you!" Dom yelled from outside the truck.

Josie laughed and Max patted her hand. "It's good to have you home."

It was, in that moment, incredibly good to be home.

Josie, unused to any kind of outside labor, much less chopping down trees, immediately got a palmful of blisters and Dom, having pulled off his hoodie, got pine sap in his hair.

"It's not funny!" Dom cried, making everything worse by touching it. "How do I get this out?"

"Cut it!" Max said with a straight face.

Dom gasped like a scandalized eighty-year old. "Never."

"It's just hair," Josie said.

"To you," he said.

"What is it to you?" Josie asked. "A crown?"

"Hockey hair," Max whispered. "He's been growing it out so that it blows behind him from underneath his helmet when he skates."

"That's why he's growing a mullet?" Josie asked. "I thought he just didn't realize how bad it looks."

"This isn't funny!" Dom yelled and then climbed into the truck and shut the door.

"It's really funny," Max said. "The kid went from not showering to, like, Hair Care King in the span of a week. Your mom still has whiplash. Come on," he said, tugging on the tree they'd just chopped down. "Help me pull this to the truck."

The bigger tree was already tied down and strapped to the truck. The smaller tree was soon wedged into the truck bed underneath the larger one.

Josie helped slam the truck gate and then braced herself, panting, against it.

"You need to get in shape," Max said.

"I am in shape," Josie cried. "Do you have any idea how many miles I walk in a day?"

"That's city shape. You need to get in country shape."

Josie rolled her eyes at him, but when she straightened up, her back protesting, she thought he might have a point. She pulled in big breaths of air that smelled so much like pine it left a taste in the back of her throat.

"Remember when Mom and I first moved here?" she asked.

"Of course." He pulled off his gloves. They were new ones, a present from Josie on his birthday. She gave him a new pair every year. It was a thing. She remembered suddenly the feel of her small hands inside of his gloves the first winter that she and Mom had been here. The soft rawhide and the warmth. They were just gloves on a cold day, but they'd made her feel so safe.

And her giving him gloves every year was a thank-you for that feeling. For making her and Mom safe. For loving them so well.

"You were building the shed. And you let me work with you even though it freaked Mom out," Josie said.

"You and I both needed to do something or we were going to lose our minds."

"Well..." She shot him an arch look, indicating he'd already lost his mind.

"Fair," he said with a smile.

"It was...it was the nicest thing anyone had done for me," she told him.

"Josie," he whispered, and Josie smiled.

"Have I said thank you?" she asked.

"Yes."

"Well, thank you again."

"It's me that needs to thank you," Max said. "You're an adult now, so maybe you'll understand it better or from a different angle, but...you saved me, too, kid."

"Well, Mom—"

"You."

"No crying, Max." He *probably* wasn't going to, but she smiled at him because she felt her own tears threaten.

They got into the truck, Dom in the back seat, having forgotten his hair emergency, seemed to be sound asleep. It was remarkable, all the things a teenage boy could do.

Max sat in the driver's seat, his hands on the wheel. But he didn't start the truck.

"What's wrong?" Josie asked, her breath making plumes in the cold air.

"I know what I'm going to say isn't going to make a difference. And I know that because nothing will make a difference until you decide that it will."

Oh lord. Could he be any more *Max*?

"Max—"

He looked over at her and she stared straight out the window, not wanting to meet his eyes. To see what he so badly wanted her to see. "It's not your fault Cameron left. It's mine."

Max had tried this before. To explain his anger when he found Cameron kissing her on her bed. Cameron's hand on her knee, Josie so bombed.

He'd pushed Cameron out the door. And Cameron, embarrassed and desperate to make the Mitchell family happy, had gone.

But none of that would have happened if she hadn't instigated the whole thing.

And it didn't change the fact that Cameron hadn't answered a single one of her emails. Or calls.

His voice was low and it was him—her found father. The man she'd decided to love as a father. It had been a choice on her part as much as it was on Max's part to love her like a daughter and the power of that...it was life-changing.

"You know it's not that simple," she said.

"Well, it's also not as simple as it all being *your* fault."

"I know."

"Then why haven't you been back?"

"Work. Life. I mean...I'm kind of a big deal." She made it a joke, hoping he'd laugh and tease her.

His silence stretched and stretched, and she knew this game of his. This silent waiting game. When she was a teenager and had come home late for curfew or smelling of beer or some other teenage infraction, Mom would lose her shit all over the place. They'd yell and push each other's buttons until it was just total pandemonium. And then once Josie had been sent to her room, Max would wait a few minutes and come up and just...stand in the doorway. Silently waiting for her to talk. And she would yell and yell and then cry...and then ultimately...she would talk.

But she didn't want to tell him how every square inch of this place was haunted with some memory of Cameron. Of them. Of how she felt about him. It was humiliating to still feel so much when he so clearly felt *nothing*. And never had.

How was she supposed to say that?

So instead she laughed and bumped her shoulder against his.

"It's not going to work," she said.

"It always works."

"I'm not fifteen."

Another beat of silence and then he started the car. "I'm here," he said. "When you're ready."

THEY DROPPED the big tree first, and just as if the whole family had been waiting for them to show up with trees, they came out with gloves on, ready to help pull it inside. Patrick, Jonah, and Daphne, too. Alice gave instructions from the stairway.

"Further left," she said, and everyone shifted in a different direction.

"Love of my life," Gabe said. "Our left or yours?"

"Oh. Mine." Alice winced and everyone shuffled in the right direction. Dom set up the industrial tree stand and Iris was there with the ropes they'd use to stand the thing up and secure it to the wall, so there wouldn't be a repeat of the tree-falling-down incident of 2012.

"Count of three," Max said.

"Wait," Alice said. "Would it be better by the windows?"

"No!" everyone yelled in unison.

"One. Two," Max said. "Three." And there was a chorus of groans and a showering of pine needles, and the tree weaved and then stood straight. And every Mitchell there cheered.

"Okay," Alice said. "Who is going to help decorate?"

And like mice, everyone scattered.

It used to be Cameron's job. Cameron and Alice for years, and then Josie joined. The three of them had spent hours on the tree. Getting the lights right. Hanging the ornaments just so. Cameron did it, in the beginning, for Alice. Because in the beginning he would do anything for Alice.

But Josie did it for Cameron. To be near him.

And at some point, she liked to believe that Cameron enjoyed being with her, too. She'd convinced herself that he felt the same way she did, but was shy. And worried about the age difference. And what the family would think.

She'd convinced herself of so much.

It's not your fault.

That was bullshit. She'd been the only other person in that room the night of her birthday. And when she'd woken up, he was gone. He'd decided to leave the only home he knew rather than stay and talk to her. Be with her. Love her.

And—more importantly—her Christmas Survival Plan was rooted firmly on her decision to not think about him.

"Josie!" Alice cried and Josie stopped in her mad dash to hide in the kitchen. Which, really, if you were going to hide from Alice was kind of a crap hiding spot.

"Busted," Helen said as she smiled and started to slide

on past her to freedom. Josie put out her hand and stopped Helen.

"Hey, you were going to tell me something last night. You didn't want me to be surprised...?"

The smile dropped from Helen's face.

"Is everything okay? You're kind of freaking me out," Josie said.

"It's fine. All is totally fine. I'll tell you later. Go help Alice."

"Come with me," Josie begged. "Please..."

"No way. You haven't been here for five years. Who do you think has been hanging all those ornaments to her exact specifications?"

Alice's exact specifications were exactly what turned something that should have been fun into a hair-pulling event. But that wasn't why Josie didn't want to do this alone, and one look at Helen's face and she knew her cousin got it.

But Helen shook her head, still unwilling to sacrifice the next few hours trying to make Alice happy.

"I will, however, save you some cookies and milk," Helen offered as a consolation prize.

"Make it cookies and wine and you're on."

"It's not even noon," Helen said, feigning shock.

"Josie!" Alice shouted.

"Cookies and wine it is," Helen said, and Josie turned around to meet her fate.

5

———

ALICE

Alice had some regrets in her life. The Snapsein wedding when she'd agreed on cupcakes for dessert. (Cupcakes, honestly. Was she ever glad that craze was over.) The soufflé misery of last year. The vegetarian Thanksgiving that was delicious, but that the old-guard Mitchell carnivores could not get their heads around.

She would have regretted her first marriage to Gabe, but without it they wouldn't have ended up here, so she couldn't quite bring herself to do it. Though she regretted her behavior at the end. The things she'd said to him. The way they'd left things...so bitter. So scorched earth.

Thank god they'd gotten a second chance.

The years she'd lost to drinking. She regretted those more than she could say.

And that night with Josie and Cameron.

She'd tried to save both of them and ended up losing them instead.

It's now or never to fix it.

Alice pushed a hand against her heart and took a deep breath.

She'd already messed this conversation up once; she didn't want to do it again.

Just let her know you don't blame her. That none of it was her fault.

That's what Gabe had told her last night. She'd gone to bed sick to her stomach over the look in Josie's eyes in the kitchen, and Gabe, as he always did, wrapped his arms around her and read her mind.

"Honey," Gabe had said, kissing her head. Her shoulder. "She was seventeen. Doing what seventeen-year-olds do. You were the adult. You and Max...you made your choices. And, frankly, so did Cameron."

She wanted to bristle. Argue in defense of the twenty-two-year-old boy she hadn't argued for hard enough at the time.

And Alice wanted to protest that she'd done all that. She'd had that conversation with Josie in the weeks that followed her birthday.

But Alice was fifty years old and she could now admit this to herself, if not out loud. When she'd had that conversation with Josie all those years ago—Alice *had* blamed the girl. Just enough that everything she'd said probably sounded like a lie.

And she was embarrassed by it. But she'd been worried and scared and so very, very angry. And she'd tried to swallow it all down and be the adult in the room but...well, she'd never been very good at that.

But it was Christmas now.

And Helen was having a baby and Josie hadn't been home in years and Alice didn't even know where Cameron was right now.

And Josie was hurting. Was still hurting.

Last night in the kitchen, seeing the tears in Josie's eyes had been a shock. That Cameron had never been in touch with her...well, shit. That spoke to a pain on Cameron's part that Alice didn't even know about. The past wasn't quite in the past for Josie, as it was for Alice. The postcards from Cameron helped. And seeing him once a year—always away from the inn, but still. Knowing he was out there and doing well. The same Cameron he'd always been. That Cameron and Josie hadn't been in touch in all these years—that was just wrong in a lot of ways.

And Alice felt pretty responsible for that.

Josie backed up out from underneath the landing with a plastic smile on her face, and Alice wanted to hug her and tell her she wasn't fooling anyone. She wanted to hug Josie and tell her everything was okay. But the girl could hardly stand to be around her; she practically jumped out of her skin every time Alice glanced her way.

It was lemon in a cut.

God, I messed this up.

Alice picked up the stepladder and started down the stairs toward the tree.

Josie followed with as many of the boxes as she could carry into the large windowed area where the tree was set up. Usually this place was full of comfortable seating, all arranged so people could look out the window or stare into the giant stone fireplace, but the couches and chairs had been pushed back to make room for the tree.

Gabe would come and take some of the chairs away and arrange the rest of them to face the Christmas tree that now dominated the space.

"You know," Alice said. "I never sit in this room after dinner unless it's Christmas."

"You like looking at the tree?"

"Yeah, it's like I wait all year for those weeks when I can turn on the Christmas lights and play 'Carol of the Bells.'"

"Oh my god," Josie said with a smile. "I forgot about you and that song."

"The single best Christmas carol ever written."

"'O Holy Night.'"

"Not even close."

"'Santa Claus Is Coming to Town'?"

"No way."

"Sung by Springsteen."

"Well...that might be second." Alice smiled at the girl, and for a second, one quick second, everything was all right.

"I can't believe you waited for me to put up the tree," Josie said, setting down the boxes of ornaments.

"Really?" Alice said. "Once we got word you were coming home, your mom put a hold on Christmas. No preparations until you got here."

"I'm sorry."

"It's not...you don't have to be sorry." Alice took a breath. "We're so happy to have you home. It's been so long, Josie."

Josie made some noise in her throat and went up for more boxes. Alice hung her head for a second.

"Do you have any guests for the holiday?" Josie asked, coming down the stairs with the last of the ornaments. Her cheer was bulletproof, and Alice understood that the poor, ravaged girl from the dark kitchen last night would not be coming out again. Not around Alice.

Unless Alice pushed.

And that seemed so mean.

And un-Christmassy.

And hard.

"We have some of the cabins booked on Christmas Eve

through the New Year," Alice answered. Happy to step back into familiar conversation. Easy conversation.

"That's nice. Is the restaurant doing Christmas dinner for everyone?"

"Not this year. Boxing Day brunch. The family is getting Christmas Eve and Christmas Day off. Helen was kind of a pest about it."

Josie laughed. "Classic Helen."

"Well, honey, you weren't much better," Alice said, as the memories rolled over her. She smiled at Josie. An easy smile. And Josie smiled back and hope blinked on in Alice's chest like the Christmas lights in her hand. "I swear the two of you and that school lunch program. The way you manipulated everyone in charge. And Cameron..."

And just saying his name ended it. The moment dissolved and Josie was still smiling, but her eyes were cold.

Alice took a deep breath, prepared to bite the bullet.

"Colored lights this year?" Josie asked, cutting in before Alice could say anything. The girl had been raised at the foot of Delia, a butter-wouldn't-melt master of nonconfrontation who Alice loved like a sister, and it was obvious Josie wasn't going to be finessed into a conversation.

Alice was going to have run right at her.

"I thought we'd change it up," Alice said and dropped the lights she'd pulled out of the box. "We need to talk, Josie."

"Sure," Josie said, looking up at Alice with a bright smile. "I suppose we need to plan some kind of baby shower for Helen. Here, or even in the city. I could host for change. That might be fun for you, right? I mean, not that I would be hosting, that's not...you know...fun for you. But being a guest. Not having to always be the one cooking and everything."

Josie was winding herself up good and Alice put her hands on her hips.

"It wasn't your fault."

"We could do a high tea," Josie said as if Alice hadn't even spoken. "Oh! At The Plaza, wouldn't that be fun?"

"Stop."

"We could rent a suite—"

"Josie, for God's sake, stop!" Alice cried and pulled the lights Josie was playing with out of her hands. Josie let the lights go but didn't look up. "It's not your fault. What happened—"

"You didn't believe that then," Josie said, and Alice winced. "I mean, you said that but... you didn't believe it."

"I was hurt, too," Alice said, lifting her arms out to the sides. It wasn't fair; she'd been supposed to be the adult in that situation. But it was the truth. And Josie deserved the truth.

Josie tried to smile, but it was a flat grimace of pain. "I'm sorry."

"You don't have to keep apologizing."

Josie shook her head and stood up straight, the little girl Alice always saw when she looked at Josie. The troubled eleven-year-old, the smart and passionate and clever teenager who kept her eye on everything. Like she was waiting for this new life she'd stepped into to be yanked away. That beautiful young woman, that girl, had grown into the woman who was walking the world with such confidence and smarts.

And the woman now—so in control. So polished and careful with a slick surface you couldn't get hold of.

Everyone was always surprised that Josie had gone into the television the way she had. Reality TV, drifting away from writing and into producing. But Alice understood.

That job combo gave the girl total control. And total control over a terrible reality television show was at least total control over something.

"I do have to keep apologizing," Josie said. "Every time I step into this place I'm reminded of everything I need to apologize for."

"No." Alice rushed to the girl, arms outstretched, desperate to hug her, but Josie flinched away so powerfully that she nearly fell over a box and Alice stopped, horrified by how wide the chasm was between them.

I can't believe I let it get this bad.

"I made Cameron leave," Josie said.

"No. Cameron made a choice—"

"Because of what I did."

"Because of what *we* did. Max and me." And that was really the truth. Alice could tell herself all day long that Cameron made the choice—and that it was the right choice looking back. But she knew the truth. She and Max hadn't given him a choice at all.

They'd made him leave.

Josie shook her head, not buying any of this.

"I want to make this right," Alice whispered.

Josie laughed, a harsh bark. "You know how you can make it right?"

"Tell me," Alice said.

"Don't pretend anymore. Don't pretend you're not mad. That you don't blame me. Everyone here pretends like I didn't ruin everything that night. You be the person who doesn't."

"Honey," Alice whispered, her voice dripping with all the sympathy she felt.

Josie shook her head. "Nope. That's not what I need from you, Alice."

"You want me to be the thing that punishes you while you're here?" *Oh god*, Alice thought, her hands shaking at her sides. Her lips trembling. "I won't be the sword you fall on, Josie. I love you too much—"

"You know, forget it. Forget it. Sorry, I can't help you decorate the tree," Josie said and turned right around.

Alice sighed so hard her knees actually gave out, and she put her hand against the back of the couch and then just sat down on the arm. Her eyes burned and her heart ached and she'd done this to the poor girl.

And she didn't know how to make it right.

"Alice?"

It was Gabe standing in the shadowy hallway. Gabe was one of those men getting better-looking with age, and he hadn't exactly been ugly when he was twenty-eight. It was enough to make a woman crazy if she thought about it. So she didn't. She just counted her blessings every day she had with the man.

"You saw all that?" she asked, embarrassed a little, but also glad he'd seen it so he knew what they were all up against with Josie.

"I did."

"I'm afraid I won't be able to make this right. That she'll leave and she'll never come back."

Gabe walked over to her, put his hand on her shoulder and pulled her up against his body. He was warm and strong and smelled familiar and safe. His hands on her body were a comfort. And Alice pressed her face to his shirt and waited for him to say the right thing. Because that was Gabe's superpower. Infallible. Unflappable. Positive in the darkest darkness.

Come on, honey, she thought. *Hit me with some bright side.*

But he was silent.

· · ·

JOSIE

Dinner was served by the light of a completely decorated Christmas tree. And Josie wanted to ask who'd finished decorating it, but after one look at Gabe and Stella, she knew Alice's husband and daughter had stepped in when Josie ran.

She'd gone back to her room in Mom and Dad's house and told Belinda, the casting agent, that maybe an all-asshole cast would be perfect. Maybe it would be exciting.

I won't be the thing that punishes you.

Yeah, Josie didn't need Alice to punish her when she had this job.

Helen came waddling into the dining room wearing a yellow sweater and black leggings, and carrying a big salad bowl. Dom followed with a big platter of parsley-flecked rice and crispy roasted potatoes. Garth and Iris followed, with Garth carrying a platter of meat.

"I will have you know," Alice said, bringing up the rear with two bottles of red wine. "I stood outside and grilled for you people."

"And for that," Jonah said, looking down at the dinner and rubbing his hands together, "you have my undying gratitude."

"You know," Daphne said. "You don't ever react to *my* dinners like this."

"I don't?" he asked, his face twisted like he was confused about something.

"You don't." Daphne lifted a white-blond eyebrow.

"Is there a way for me to get out of this conversation without being in trouble?"

"Yeah. You can promise to cook."

"Done," Jonah said and leaned over to kiss Daphne.

"How are things at Haven House?" Josie asked as they all sat down to a beautiful Greek feast. The green salad was full of chunks of salty white feta cheese and the pita had been brushed with olive oil and toasted over the fire. Josie lived in one of the most exciting food cities in the world, but when you grew up with Alice cooking for you, it was all a little anti-climactic.

She made it seem so easy.

"It's going pretty well," Jonah said, looking over at Daphne who nodded in agreement. "We've brought in a few more teachers for both the mothers and the children. Daphne's work program at the farm has been at capacity since we started."

"I've hired two full-time employees from the program and we've been able to move the mothers and their kids into permanent housing in town."

"That's amazing," Josie said. Haven House had been built while she was in high school and the program was up and running by her first year at college. They brought single mothers and their kids out of hard environments with few opportunities and started them off with a vacation in a beautiful inn with plenty of green space and even an indoor swimming pool. And then, slowly, they introduced programs on how to understand basic finances and their legal rights, as well as art and basic home repair, and then slowly branched into things like job training.

"We miss you, though," Jonah said.

"Ha! Well, free labor and all that." Josie felt Alice's eyes across the room and just did not feel comfortable taking compliments in front of her.

"No, you were so good with those writing courses for the moms and the kids. You really struck a nerve."

Josie's birth father had been a violent guy—never to her, just to her mom—and Josie, when she worked at Haven House that summer, had really felt the ramifications of that. A lot of those kids had had the same kind of crappy experience.

"Remember when Cameron did that cooking class with the children?" Gabe asked, laughing. Josie felt her throat close up.

"The Riverview kitchen was the only kitchen big enough for all of them," Jonah said.

"Yeah." Gabe smiled at his brother. "I've heard that before."

"Cameron was cleaning flour out of the tile for weeks," Alice said.

So was I, Josie thought. *And I taught that class with him. And when the kids opened the wrong end of the flour bag and the bowl fell on the floor, it was the two of us. We hit heads trying to grab the flour and he put his fingers around my wrist and my pulse beat against his skin and I was sure—sure—I was just going to die from him being so close.*

She'd wished, like any sixteen-year-old girl deeply in love with a twenty-one-year-old man might wish, that he would apply the pressure to her wrist that would pull her closer to him. And then, when she was a breath away, he'd smile his half smile, hiding that crooked tooth he was embarrassed about, and press those smiling lips to hers.

She'd wished that wish so many times it was nearly a prayer.

Helen set a very big glass of wine down in front of Josie.

"Whoa." Josie laughed. "You trying to get me drunk?"

"You're drinking for two tonight," Helen said with what seemed like a nervous smile.

"The second person is you, I take it?"

Helen nodded glancing backward at the door and then over at her parents.

"You all right?" Josie asked. She took a sip of the red wine and then another. She'd managed, so far, to keep the memories of Cameron at arm's length. But she could feel them hovering tonight. Close enough to touch.

"Fine," Helen said. "But look, whatever happens tonight, I just want you to know that everything is going to be okay."

"You're freaking me out, Helen," Josie said, turning to face her cousin more fully.

"Alice?" Grandmother Iris was looking over her shoulder at the tree. "Did you do something different with the tree this year?" she asked.

"No. I mean, the lights are on a timer," Alice said, putting green salad on her plate. "But I did that last year."

"I think..." Patrick got to his feet, and over his shoulder Josie saw the branches of the tree shimmy. "...maybe the tree had a stowaway."

"What are you talking about, Dad?" Max asked, leaning forward so he could see the tree too.

A squirrel poked its head out of the branches.

"Holy shit!" Dom swore. Mom smacked the back of his head.

Max, Gabe, and Jonah all got to their feet and the sound of all the chairs scraping back startled the squirrel, who jumped off the branch onto the floor.

Alice screamed and jumped away from the table. "It's the racoons all over again!"

Mom stepped back too, but she had the good sense to grab the wine bottle and a glass as she went. Iris, Stella, and Garth were freaking out. Which also sent the squirrel into a tizzy, and the poor animal darted left and then right toward the fireplace.

"Don't let it—" Max shouted, but the squirrel must have thought better of his plans and took an immediate right and jumped up onto the table.

Everyone screamed.

"Jesus," Max said. "Someone open the front door."

The squirrel ran right down the center of the table, over all the food, through the salad bowl, sending lettuce flying.

"Come on!" Alice cried, throwing her arms up in the air.

"I got it, Dad," Josie said, walking backward toward the door. Without looking she opened it, hoping the cold air might lure the squirrel outside.

Max tried to scare the squirrel in the direction of the front entry, but all the squirrel did was knock over a candle. Helen, acting fast, threw her glass of water over the flame. And the squirrel, instead of heading for the front door, went running and then leaped off the end of the table toward the kitchen.

"Not my kitchen!" Alice cried and went running after it.

Dom and Max followed and from the kitchen there was the sound of glass shattering, and Alice swearing a blue streak.

The chill from the open front door behind Josie got to be too much, and she imagined other squirrels in the forest, hearing the plight of their brother, might come charging in to save the day. And Alice would have a conniption.

So she turned to shut the door.

But there was a man standing there.

Tall and wide, with a backpack over his shoulder. He looked like he'd walked himself here over a million miles, or perhaps through a bunch of years. He had a beard and a bright red hat pulled low on his head.

"Hi," he said, and his voice sent chills down Josie's spine. Across all her skin.

No. It can't be.

At almost the exact same time she thought, *Please. Please let it be him.*

And then he smiled, his half smile hiding the crooked tooth he was embarrassed about.

"Cameron." His name tumbled past her numb lips.

"Long time no see, Josie," he said.

6

———

CAMERON
In Italy, four summers ago, before YouTube changed everything, Cameron had been broke as broke could be. So he'd agreed to work for room and board for this absolute asshole of an artist. He was a glassblower high in the hills of Tuscany. And Cameron had worked like a dog for Carlo in his sweltering hot workshop and then ended up having to cook for the guy, too. Which wasn't such a chore—the guy pressed his own olive oil and he had chickens and goats, and lemon trees and rosemary grew wild in the yard.

One afternoon, after the ovens were turned off and the hills had cooled down, and Carlo had finished his second, or more likely third, bottle of wine, he'd grunted at Cameron to accompany him.

With another bottle of wine and the juice glasses Carlo like to drink from, they gathered up the week's successes— the glass pieces Carlo hadn't smashed off the blow pipe— and carried them in their arms up the crumbling stone steps to the top of the hill behind the house. Lizards scattered and grasshoppers bounced out of their way.

The air had smelled like rosemary and sunshine, and the light was syrup poured over the hills, and it was—for a moment—worth the burns and the work and the crap mattress in the guest room.

And then Carlo, taking a great swig of wine, started tossing the glass over the side of the hill onto the flat patio stones below where they shattered. Spectacularly.

"What are you doing?" Cameron had asked.

Carlo explained—in a voice that was passionate but slurred—that the glass was not perfect. And therefore worthless.

Carlo lit a smoke and reached for the pieces in Cameron's arms. Cameron, exhausted and burned and a little drunk on the Tuscan sunlight, but just figuring out who he was as a chef and a man, tried to hold onto the lime green squiggle pieces in his arms even harder.

Because he was realizing that perfection was cold. And destructive. And he was about the imperfect. The messy and flawed. The welcoming and warm.

But the old man did not give up and there was actually a tussle. One of the pieces slipped out of Cameron's hands and fell onto the rough stones they were standing on, and for one second it really seemed like it wasn't going to shatter.

It held its shape despite the awful cracking noise.

Phew, he remembered thinking. *I saved it.*

And then it collapsed into pieces.

The scene in the Riverview was exactly like that moment.

No one said anything.

No one moved.

No one was even breathing. They were frozen.

And for a second it was like this wasn't even happening at all.

Am I dreaming this?

Josie, standing near the door, looked like she wanted the floor to open up and swallow her whole, and he understood that desire so well he nearly said something about it. Nearly made a joke. Like everything that had happened between them hadn't, and they were just the kids they'd been.

But then she turned away as if looking at him was too damn hard.

And he felt the echo of the slick shame he'd spent years dealing with. Faint, sure, but there all the same.

And Helen—who, it was good to see, was actually pregnant and not just throwing that card around willy-nilly, winced and lifted her hand in a tiny wave.

And the room absolutely exploded.

"Cameron!" Everyone was talking at once, yelling, running toward the door. Of course Alice was there first. He'd counted on that. Like walking into hostile territory and seeing one familiar face.

"What...what are you doing here?" Alice asked, holding onto him so hard he could feel the knuckles of her fingers wrapped in his shirt.

"A pregnant blackmailer was involved," he said, smiling at everyone lined up over Alice's shoulder.

"I can't believe it," Alice whispered, and he could feel her tears building in the hitch of her shoulders. "Why didn't you warn me?"

"Come on, Alice," he whispered in her ear. "This is hard enough."

She sucked in a breath and stepped away, nothing but smiles. Helen was next. Delia. Patrick and Iris. The kids, none of whom were really kids anymore. Gabe. Jonah and Daphne. Garth, a teenager, tried to help him with his backpack.

"It's heavy," Cameron warned him.

"It's a backpack," Garth said with all the assurance of a teenager. *Don't tell me what I don't know.* Cameron remembered that feeling so well.

"All right," Cameron said and shrugged out of the bag, which immediately toppled Garth over the edge of a chair.

"Holy crap, what's in that thing?" Garth asked, wrestling it down to the ground.

"My whole life," Cameron answered. Which sounded dramatic and like an exaggeration, but really wasn't.

There were more hugs and some tears. With every hug, he found himself pulling deeper inside of his skin. Farther away from anyone's touch.

An old survival skill.

But then there was Max.

And there weren't enough survival skills in the world to handle Max.

"Son," he said in a low murmur, and Cameron flinched just as Max came in for a hug. And the flinch froze Max in his place and maybe...well, maybe that was fine. For the best.

They were men now, no matter how much Max might want to "son" him. And what had happened between them in the past made it a little hard to hug the man now. He still remembered the taste of shame in the back of his throat, the way he'd been unable to look Max in the eye that night.

Shit.

He was a man now, and the choices that had been made were all his own. And truthfully, he was grateful in a lot of ways for how that whole thing had shaken out.

But the memory was still a bad one.

He was doing his best to squash an older survival skill. Learned in his father's house. From his father's fists.

Anger. Anger at all of them. At himself. If he could just be angry he wouldn't feel ashamed about that night. Or pained by the years. Or shocked at all the silver in Alice's hair.

Or pierced right through the gut by Josie.

He was trying not to notice her, where she lingered on the edge of the crowd of Mitchells. The place she'd occupied for a long time. Hovering at the periphery but never pushing her way inside. It was one of the things that had bound them together when they were kids. Belonging, sure. But not really.

Stop.

He took a deep breath so he could let go of the anger.

Nope. No way. That way lies madness.

It seemed crucial that he treat her the same as he treated every other Mitchell, but that was so difficult he found himself ignoring her. And that was easier. In so many ways.

So he stopped giving himself a headache watching her out of the corner of his eye, but he could still feel her. Like there was a string stretched between them, and he felt the tug and pull the further away she got.

This was a feeling he had forgotten about. The feeling that dogged him the first few months after he left, before he headed for Europe, putting Josie, the Riverview, and that night a million miles behind him.

It had taken a while before the first thought he'd had upon waking up was *not* about Josie. Or the Riverview. These people.

But it had happened. He'd moved on.

"You came," Helen said, smiling up at him.

"You made it pretty clear I had to." He looked down at her belly. "How are you feeling?"

"Great."

"Where's Evan?" He'd met Helen's guy a while back. They'd all been in Washington, DC, at the time. They were doing some lobby work and he had been in the city to interview an urban farmer, but then ended up staying because he and the urban farmer had fallen into her bed for about a month.

Cameron liked Evan as a person and he really liked him as a partner for Helen. He was a grounding force for that girl, whose natural state was electric.

"He's been delayed," she said. "But he promises he'll be here by Christmas Eve."

"He better," Cameron said. Alice was back from the kitchen bringing piles of food, bright eyed but not crying. She set down the serving bowls and then grabbed him, ushering him toward the table. Her arm around his waist like a steel girder.

Her message was clear—you are not getting away from me.

"You must be hungry. Are you hungry?" she asked.

It was the question of his teenage years. God, the food she'd fed him. Stuffing him with potatoes and fresh green beans and plums and cheese and cakes made from scratch with love. He'd eaten it all. Every bit. All the time.

So used to starving he hadn't even realized how hungry he was.

"What...happened here?" he asked, looking down at the messy table, serving bowls on their sides, forks on the floor. Total mayhem.

"There was a squirrel in the tree," Alice said, pointing at the giant Christmas tree in front of the windows.

"Oh my god, it's the racoons all over again," Cameron said, remembering the racoons that had invaded the party tent the night before the very first wedding ever held at the Riverview.

"What a night that was," Alice said.

"I don't think it was that bad," Gabe said with a smile just for Alice.

He had a physical reaction to Gabe and Alice, same as when he was a kid. A tension down his back, his hands curling into fists. As a teenager in constant survival mode, with nothing but anger and fear to feed him, the love and respect they had for each other had seemed fake. And it had literally made him angry. And when that love and affection had been spread his way he fought it with every part of his being.

Until Max somehow convinced him it was real. Something he could count on.

And he didn't regret giving up that fight, but perhaps—if he hadn't let them all the way in—he might have been able to protect himself a little bit better.

"Well, it probably won't be the last wild animal loose in this place," Max said, coming to stand next to him. Cameron stepped away just enough that he didn't feel Max there. Couldn't see him out of the corner of his eye. Could, in fact, pretend he wasn't there at all.

His father had had the good grace to never be a decent man. Much less a father. But this guy? Max? He'd taught Cameron everything he understood about being a man.

Josie stepped up to the place across the table from him.

And he made the stupid mistake of looking at here. Right at her. It was like staring into the face of the sun. The girl she'd been was still there. Still recognizable. The freck-les. The green eyes. Her wild red hair had changed to auburn and it caught the light behind her and made her glow. She was still tall and thin, and he wanted to ask if she still ran road races every spring. He'd done that with her for a few years because the training runs were such a good chance to be close to her. God, what a fool he'd been. He *hated* running.

She was wearing black jeans and a silky black shirt, and he'd seen that New York uniform every time Netflix or YouTube brought him into their offices. She was in television somewhere in the city. And every time he'd said yes to those visits, he'd had to force himself not to imagine running into her on the subway. Or in some bodega getting coffee. And he hadn't. All day he'd walk around not thinking about her.

But at night he would dream unhinged dreams about her.

Dreams that made him uncomfortable. Dreams about anger and sex.

He'd wake up hard and grieving.

And angry.

He felt it now as he sat across the table from her. The attraction and the loss and the anger. Wanting something he couldn't have. And shouldn't even want anymore. Wanting something he'd hurt.

He took one last glance at her face, to memorize the grown-up version of the girl he'd been so wild for.

She was crying and trying to hide it.

She was crying and trying to stop.

She was crying.

Because of me.

And he would have stayed no matter how uncomfortable he was. How angry and resentful. How hurt.

But he wasn't going to stay and hurt her.

Shit. Just...shit.

He looked at Helen. "I'm sorry," he murmured.

And he turned and left.

The Mitchell family was quiet behind him. Speechless. The reverse, maybe, of the shattering glass of before. He'd leave—again. And everything would go back the way it was supposed to be.

And he grabbed his winter coat, swung his heavy bag over his shoulder, and headed outside. He'd rented a car for this trip, thinking in the back of his head that he would need a getaway option.

And it sat at the side of the road, a nondescript dark sedan. He'd never been so happy about the decisions that past him had made.

He fished the keys out of his pocket and hit the fob.

There was the sound of feet behind him and he didn't turn to see who had followed him.

Helen, maybe. The instigator.

Alice? He'd write her an email, explaining everything. She'd understand. For a long time she'd had her own sharp edges that kept people from getting too close.

Josie?

He hoped not. Couldn't imagine it. He'd spent the first year of his exile imagining her finding him in his tiny apartments and hectic jobs. In Baltimore and Wyoming. San Francisco and Vancouver.

All while deleting pictures of her from his phone. Ignoring her emails.

He'd had to leave the continent to leave that daydream behind.

"Cameron?"

Jesus. It was Max.

Cameron sighed and stopped. Not because he wanted to

talk to the guy. But because he knew Max wasn't going to let up and this whole thing could end with Cameron running him over with the car or some bullshit.

He turned to face Max. "Max, I think we can both admit it was a mistake for me to come. I never should have—"

Max just kept walking. Not stopping, and Cameron felt the way he had that night, like Max might hit him. And he wasn't a boy anymore, and if it was going to come to that, to a god damn fistfight with his old mentor, then—fine. Weirder shit had happened.

He shrugged out of his backpack and changed up his stance. Max was still big and strong, and he had that ice-hard I've-killed-a-man edge to him that had always frankly terrified Cameron, but Cameron had been broke and home-less on the streets of Bangkok on more than one occasion.

He knew how to handle himself.

"Jesus, Max!" he shouted as the old guy got close, and he threw out an arm, a loosely gathered fist because, honest to god, he didn't want to hit the man. But Max grabbed him by the shoulders, his dark eyes searching Cameron's, and Cameron tried to step back but Max wouldn't let him.

"I'm so sorry," Max said, and wrapped his arms around Cameron.

He held himself still—shades of the glass breaking—before pushing at the guy's chest.

"Max—"

"I'm so goddamn sorry, and if I was a better man—"

"Stop!" Cameron said, but Max just kept hugging him and talking. Cameron could only stand there and take it.

"I'll leave," Max said. "Just come back inside. Alice is ready to burn the place down and Helen is crying. I'll make myself scarce."

Cameron slumped in the man's embrace, enough that

Max must have gotten the sense that Cameron wasn't going to fight him anymore and let him go.

Cameron looked over Max's shoulder at the inn. Alice was standing in the doorway. He could see how anxious she was. He could feel it, practically. She was the only mom he'd ever known, really. Anything good that grew in his life, he could trace the roots back to her.

To Max, too, in a lot of ways.

It wasn't comfortable. But there it was.

"It just seems…"

"Like a lot?" Max finished.

Cameron huffed. "You guys are always a lot," he said. "But this maybe…maybe it's just too much. It's Christmas, and I think I'm a bad memory—"

Max sucked in a breath. "I'm so sorry you think that." He shook his head, and to Cameron's total and utter shock the former cop seemed to be about to cry. "Because you're not."

"That night is," Cameron said. He would not be put off by platitudes. He wanted to say *Josie is in there crying*. But he couldn't even say her name.

Max shook his head, so sad. "Not…for the reasons you think. Everyone regrets what happened. All of us. And if you come in…"

"We're going to be one big happy family?" Cameron asked.

"Yes."

"I wasn't part of the family, Max. I was an employee."

"You were much more than that, Cameron. So much more. And even if you don't remember that, I do. Alice does. Everyone in there does. Josie—"

Cameron lifted his hand and Max, thank god, shut his mouth.

Cameron glanced up at the tops of the trees, the slate-gray sky above them. There was going to be snow soon. He could smell it. Max had taught him that. How the air changed in advance of weather. It had felt, learning it, like a stupid thing. But in his life on the road it had become a superpower.

I owe them so much.

"It's Christmas, son—"

"Stop," Cameron said. "Stop. I'll come in. I'll stay for dinner. Past that...we'll go meal by meal, okay?"

Max blinked back his tears. "Meal by meal sounds familiar."

"But you don't call me son. Not ever again."

Max nodded solemnly, like he understood it was the price of the past.

Cameron reached down for his backpack, but Max got there first.

"Good god, no wonder Garth fell over. What do you keep in there?"

"My home," Cameron said. Max looked at him like he was joking, but he wasn't.

He'd lost the only home he'd ever had, really. The only family.

He lived his whole life now making sure he didn't have another one to lose.

7

———

JOSIE

Her first season working as an intern for the show had been the kind of season where everything went wrong. And since it had been her first year, she'd had no perspective on it. Josie had thought that things like the set catching on fire, and the costume department going on strike, and a stomach flu—the kind that created explosive diarrhea—burning its way through the cast were all normal.

She'd met every problem with the grim determination to control it. The way she couldn't control any other thing.

Every season after that first season had been easier—which might be a part of why she stayed.

The rest of the night that Cameron came back to the Riverview was like that. After the shock of seeing him, the painful gut-clenching reaction to his obvious inability to look her in the eye, it wasn't so bad.

When he walked away from the table and grabbed his things, clearly leaving, it hadn't even registered in the atmosphere of shock in her brain.

When he and Max walked back in like nothing was really wrong, she didn't know what to feel.

Relief? Dread?

So she used the great coping mechanism she always used.

She worked.

She cleared the dishes the squirrel had upset. She brought out new place settings. New silverware. When the oven timer went off and fresh bread was baked, she took care of it. Brought it out, sliced and wrapped in the cloth napkins that fresh bread was always wrapped in here at the Riverview.

She filled water glasses.

"Sit," Helen urged when Josie jumped up to go grab a bottle of wine. "I'll get it."

But Josie was already halfway to the kitchen.

The kitchen was still dark and quiet. The smell of the dinner Alice had worked so hard on lingered, and the pots and pans were piled up, waiting for whichever family members were on the clean-up crew to come in and take care of them and probably another bottle of wine. Or two.

They'd bring Cameron in here and make him sit at the counter and not lift a finger as he told them more stories about his travels.

Out in the dining room it was a regular story time.

And she wanted to listen to every word and ask seven hundred follow-up questions.

You traveled with a Mongolian nomadic tribe for a month?

What does yak blood taste like?

What did you make for Prince Harry and Meghan?

Why were you arrested in France?

Did you miss us?

Did I ever cross your mind?

But the obvious answer to those last two questions was *no*.

The swinging door to the dining room opened as Josie took two bottles of white wine from the fridge. For the second her back was turned to the door, she foolishly hoped the footsteps belonged to Cameron.

"Josie." It was Helen. Looking pregnant and contrite. Josie had a million things she could yell, but she swallowed them and smiled.

"I've got the wine," she said, like she didn't understand what Helen wanted.

"I'm sorry," Helen whispered.

"For what?"

Helen shook her head and crossed the dark kitchen toward Josie.

"I'm just getting the wine," Josie said, and she side-stepped Helen as she reached out.

"I thought it would be happy," Helen said. "The two of you back here like this. I thought..."

What? He'd forgiven me? I'd forgotten him?

"Are you happy?" Josie asked, the words coming out harder than she'd intended. Meaner. It was like a crack in the wall, and the rest of her darker feelings rushed her, clamoring to be let out. Words she'd never said wanted to be said. Things she hardly remembered feeling.

"No." Helen said, looking like the guiltiest, saddest pregnant girl who ever lived.

And it only made Josie angrier.

Josie stood still under the force of what she wanted to say. Scream at her cousin and best friend.

"You were both so young and you've both gone on to do such amazing things and you never...you never talk about him and he never talks about you and I thought..." Helen sighed. "I thought it would be happy."

Through the swinging door came a roar of laughter.

"Stop!" Alice shrieked. "You're making that up!"

"I'm serious," Cameron said, and there was more laughter.

"It is happy," she told Helen.

But she knew at once that she wasn't going back in there. She'd take the farm truck back to her parents' place and... she didn't know past that.

Work?

Leave?

Hide?

"Take these to the table, would you?" She handed the wine bottles to Helen.

"Where are you going?"

"Back to my parents'."

"But—" Helen looked over her shoulder at the door, the family and happiness on the other side.

"Tell them I got a work call," Josie said. They'd believe it. And it wasn't even a lie. Her phone had been buzzing in her pocket all night.

She grabbed her keys from the hook by the door, and without even her winter coat, stepped outside into the brittle cold and made her escape.

8

CAMERON
The headache woke him up. The headache and the sun slicing through the window because he'd forgotten to close the curtains.

As a rule Cameron didn't drink. Lessons from his father and all that. But when Helen had come back into the dining room with two bottles of wine and the news that Josie had gotten a work call. Well...he'd jumped headfirst into one of those bottles.

And then Alice broke out the good whiskey and poured him a glass while he did the dishes.

He wouldn't let her help do the dishes.

She didn't join him in a drink.

And he remembered the promise she'd made to him so many years ago. That she would stop drinking. It had been the very first promise an adult had made to him and kept. Which, if you were a kid like he'd been, was revolutionary. He'd grown used to being disappointed and forgotten. But in that moment, Alice—practically a stranger, relatively speaking—had put him first. It had been the start of who they'd become. This bond that was more than friendship, but just left of parenthood.

Last night he'd had to look away, plunge his hands into the hot, soapy water to distract himself from the ache that memory gave him.

I should go.

It was honestly his first thought.

Before everyone woke up, he should just pack and leave a note and hit the road. He'd been invited to spend Christmas in Montreal with an ice skater he met two years ago. He and Ingrid kept in touch and spent holidays together when she was single and he had nowhere else to go.

He cooked. She trained. They had extremely athletic sex. It was not a bad arrangement.

If he stayed, things would get messy. That was just the reality of staying anywhere. But here the threat of messiness was...well, it was more of a guarantee. With Max.

With Josie.

God. The dreams he'd had of her last night. Against his leg, his dick twitched.

Calm down.

Though there was a sort of poetry to masturbating to the idea of her in the same room where he'd done it seven million times.

He still wanted her. Maybe that shouldn't be a surprise.

Not just the idea of her or the memory—but her. The flesh and blood woman sitting across from him at that table, unable to make eye contact.

It felt inevitable. And reckless. And...mean? He wasn't sure about that. But there was an edge to his desire for her that hadn't been there when they were young. He wanted to take all of their innocence and smash it. And all that restraint he'd shown for so long? He wanted to tie her up with it.

Oh god. *That* image.

He wanted to make good on all the promise their relationship had had. He wanted to be sweet, so sweet. The sweetest, like they were still virgins.

And he wanted to hurt her. And be hurt by her. He wanted raw and filthy and wrong—and then he wanted to walk away. From the boy he'd been. The girl she'd been.

His messed-up memories of that night.

Yeah. I gotta get out of here.

It just wasn't worth it. He'd shown his face. Told some stories. Hugged some people. He could leave with a clear conscience. *Thanks, Helen, for the invite. It's been fun, but I can't stay.*

He would text her that from the road.

Texts from the road were his calling card. He never stayed long in any place, and when he left it was no one's business but his.

Cameron sighed and sat up, running his hands through his hair. He'd spent a year getting made fun of for his man bun so he tried to avoid that length now. But it wasn't always easy to find a barber, or sometimes even a pair of scissors, in his life on the road less taken.

It was too short for a bun, too shaggy for Alice's kitchen.

He pulled on a pair of loose sweatpants and a T-shirt. Found a pair of socks that were mostly clean (laundry was always an issue when you only had a few of everything) packed up the rest of his stuff and headed downstairs.

The lodge was beautiful and never more so than at Christmas. The wooden walls and high ceilings were made for pine trees and blinking Christmas lights and roaring fires in the fireplace.

At the foot of the stairs he sighed, bag in hand.

Alice was making breakfast. He could smell coffee and baking bread. He could hear her humming off-key, taking bacon out of the fridge.

For him. He knew she was doing it for him.

And he might have adopted a love 'em and leave 'em attitude over the last seven years, but he couldn't do it to Alice. Again.

He took a deep breath. Cool air. Christmas tree. Faint woodsmoke from hundreds of fires like last night's. The smell of the Riverview Inn at Christmas. In a few hours Alice would put the mulling spices to simmer on the back of the stove and it would smell so good you could take a bite out of the air.

Stay, he thought. *Just...stay. For a little while.* What could it hurt?

And he put down his bag. Another lesson learned from his years on the road—he could leave anytime. Once he'd let that be his code of conduct, it was pretty freeing. Stay for a while. Go when things got too tense.

Owe no one anything.

He pulled his phone and his little tripod out of his backpack. The coffeemaker was in there, that one Josie gave him. Blackened by a million fires. Beat up from the time he'd dropped it off Half Dome in Yosemite.

The number of times he'd thought about replacing it... countless. He'd been sent other camping stoves, other coffeemakers, and he used none of them.

With a hard jerk he pulled the drawstring taut on the top of the bag, hiding his life from view.

"Hey," he said, walking into the kitchen to find Alice exactly where he expected to find her. Standing at the stainless-steel counter, cookbook in front of her, coffee cup in hand.

"Good morning," Alice said with a smile. Sunbeams highlighted the years that had passed, but in a beautiful way. Almost holy.

He sighed at his melodrama. That was the problem with him and this place. Why really it had been good he'd left. His attachment, his perspective, was unreasonable. He'd never been able to see these people clearly. It was all hero worship in his head.

And lust for a girl who could never be his.

"How are you feeling?"

"Like I need a cup of coffee."

"You know where the pot is," she said.

He poured himself a cup and sat down on one of the stools on the edge of the stainless-steel island.

"What...what are you doing?" she asked as he set up the phone and the tripod.

"I think you know what I'm doing."

"Cameron."

"Five questions, Alice. We've never done it."

"Oh my god," she sighed. "What's my hair look like?"

She had a wild rooster tail on top and it was seriously hilarious. "Fantastic."

Scowling at him, she patted down her rooster tail.

"You ready?" he asked.

"No."

He grinned and pressed the record button. "Alice Mitchell," he said. "Head chef of the Riverview Inn and the person who taught me everything I know about peeling potatoes. Five questions. Ready?"

"No."

"What's your comfort food?"

"Tomato soup and grilled cheese."

"Something you'd never eat again?"

"Horse sashimi. If I'd known what it was the first time, I wouldn't have had it."

"Best thing about Christmas?"

"A house full of family and the first bite of the first sugar cookie."

"Someone dead you wish you could have a meal with?"

"Your mother."

Stunned, he didn't realize what she'd said at first. And then it was his turn to scowl and he turned off the camera.

"That's not funny," he said.

"I wasn't trying to be. She died when you were so little and I imagine her sometimes, wherever she is, worrying about what became of you with your dad. And I would like to tell her that you are all right. You turned out pretty amazing."

Again, the urge to leave was powerful, and like she knew that, she did what she'd always done when he wanted to leave.

"I have a job for you," she said as she laid bacon down on her pan in even strips.

"I figured."

She shot him a smile and he found himself smiling back, and the thing about his mom faded into the distance.

"We're making lasagna, focaccia, and salad."

"Easy enough."

"For two hundred people."

His jaw dropped.

She laughed and patted his shoulder. "I missed that face."

"Are you serving that many here?"

"No. We're delivering it tomorrow to the families at

Haven House and then taking what's left to the Methodist Church."

"How far are you?" he asked, and because he'd learned kitchen management from this woman, he was already making lists.

"I've made coffee," she said with a smile.

He laughed. "Well, put me to work. I'm at your disposal."

She sighed and leaned over to pat his cheek. "I missed this face."

"I missed you, too," he said. More than he'd realized.

She sighed and looked up at his hair. "What's happening..." She twirled a finger toward his head. "...with that?"

"My hair? It's personal expression."

"I'm all for personal expression but that's a problem."

"You have a hair net?"

She shook her head.

"How about a haircut? Anyone around here good with scissors? I thought Stella—"

"Josie used to cut your hair," Alice said, turning away from him to check the bread in the oven. "Remember?"

Remember?

He'd put those memories away, having abused them more than was good for a man.

"She'd sit you outside and put a sheet over your shoulders." Alice took out the bread she'd baked, poking at the crust before putting it back in. "You'd look like you got in an accident with garden shears—remember?"

"Yes," he said tightly.

Alice was silent and he made the mistake of looking over at her.

Here it comes...

"We really fucked up both of you that night," Alice said. She shook her head, her face pale and pinched.

"I'm not fucked up," he said. Though even as he said it, he wondered...maybe it was a lie. Maybe? Who lives all this time out of a backpack? All he knew for sure was that memories of Josie were so painful he just didn't think them anymore.

Like they'd been erased.

"You're saying..." He couldn't say her name out loud. "...*she* is?"

"She hasn't been back here in five years," Alice said, looking over at him with damp eyes. "You left that day and you never came back. How is that not fucked up?"

"You and I saw each other," he said, getting to his feet. "France that summer and San Francisco for Easter."

"But you didn't come back *here*," Alice said. "The Riverview was your home and I took it—"

"You didn't," he said. "You didn't take anything."

"Then Max did."

"Alice. Stop. I left. I made the choice. Me."

She opened her mouth like she wanted to argue some more, and frankly, if it was going to be like that—he would leave.

The back door swung open and there, suddenly, was Josie. As if their talking about her had summoned her. She had her laptop and the charging cable was around her shoulders, like she'd killed big game and was bringing it home for the whole cave.

When she saw them, a breathless moment of panic flashed across her face, and then the fakest fake smile spread over her mouth.

It was like looking at a stranger. A familiar stranger.

He got very occupied pulling his camera out of the tripod.

"You're coming because of the Wi-Fi?" Alice asked, the

emotional woman of a second ago gone, and it was just Alice there, sipping coffee and taking the bread out of the oven.

"Yeah, the house—"

"Is a dead zone. Come on in. You want coffee?"

"No. I'm all right," Josie said. Her eyes met his and bounced away, and the smile on her face became so sharp it looked painful.

Standing there, she looked like New York. Fully plugged in and wearing black. Buzzing with a kind of frenetic energy. Even at 8 a.m. Too thin. Like all the extra that a person needed to feed a life outside of work was gone. And it was just work.

He glanced away, embarrassed to have noticed so much. Or, really, to think that he knew anything about her.

Her phone rang and she dug it out of her pants. "Yes. Yes. I need another second. No, I'm not on the moon. It's just...gimme a sec."

Josie raced through the kitchen, cables trailing, phone pressed to her ear.

When the door swung shut behind her, the kitchen was silent. Too silent. He could practically hear Alice's brain turn.

"You should go talk to her," Alice said. Slices of bacon began to sizzle in the pan and Alice poked at them with the long-tined fork she'd been using to fry bacon for as long as he'd known her.

"She seems pretty busy," he said with a laugh, pretending to be relaxed. Pretending the idea of talking to her didn't make him ache. Pretending he didn't owe her... something. An explanation. An apology.

"Hmm," Alice said.

"What does that mean?" he asked with a laugh. Alice's *hmms* had a whole subversive language all their own.

"Used to be a time you guys wouldn't shut up."

"Well, I'm not sure we have much to talk about anymore."

"Really?"

"Yeah...I mean...we went pretty different directions."

Alice actually gaped at him.

"What?"

"I think you went in exactly the same direction, just in different ways."

He shook his head and crossed over to the counter where he'd learned how to peel potatoes—lots of potatoes—and make a piecrust and season a pork roast. Where he'd made dumplings and friendships.

"I think she needs someone to talk to," Alice said quietly. "I think...I think something is wrong with her."

Don't care. Don't. This is a path you do not want to take.

But the word came out anyway. "Wrong?"

She shrugged. "It's just...a hunch. You gonna help me with this dinner?"

"It's why I'm here," he said, grateful they weren't talking about Josie anymore. Grateful to be put to work and kept busy.

And soon he was mincing garlic and browning sausage.

Aware, every second, that Josie was just through the doorway.

JOSIE

Crisis averted.

Josie blew out a breath.

So much energy, she thought. *So much energy, and for what?*

To keep a contestant struggling with an addiction problem on the show because she has a million Instagram followers? They'd agreed to pay for a sobriety coach and Josie had put her foot down that it would be a sobriety coach the production company chose. They'd fallen for that before. The previous year a contestant had brought a "sobriety coach" who was actually his dealer.

She felt a question—the question—the one she didn't like, looming at the edge of her consciousness. *What am I doing?*

She started a new email to Dan and Joanne, her *I Do/I Don't* bosses.

You know, she wrote, *we could actually tackle issues of addiction if we changed the focus of the show to something along the lines of my pitch. I know that you're discussing the merits of my idea and I can't tell you how much I appreciate it. And I'm here to answer any other questions you have or work over some of the ideas. It's a way to do something bigger. Something better. We should schedule a talk in the New Year.*

She hit Send, buoyed again by the strength of her idea. The power of pulling them out of the gutter and putting the show—and herself—on a different path.

"Josie?" It was Alice bellowing on her way in from the kitchen. "I need you."

"What do you need?" she asked, turning to look over the edge of the sofa to see Alice come in with Cameron behind her. His hair was long. She hadn't realized it the previous night. It came down to his chin. He looked a little like Leonardo DiCaprio in the Titanic movie.

And thin gray sweatpants.

And a body with muscles that filled out the sleeves and shoulders of his shirt.

Good god, it just wasn't fair what the years had done to Cameron. They'd taken a good-looking kid and turned him into a heart-stopping man.

"I need you to do something with him!" Alice said, pointing at Cameron.

And now...honestly, objectively, that wasn't dirty. It was just Josie and her dirty mind and the gray sweatpants that made those words seem dirty.

But Cameron's cheeks turned pink and he couldn't meet her eyes, and that made it all worse. Better?

She wasn't sure.

"His hair!" Alice said. "The boy's dropping hair in my tomato sauce and I can't have it."

"If you have a ponytail holder," he said to Josie, "we'll let you get back to work."

"I don't. But Iris must be around here—"

"Cut it," Alice said. "Cut his hair. Like you used to."

"Oh...that's a terrible idea," Josie said.

"Well, it's the only way he's working in my kitchen. Gabe's clippers are still in the back bathroom. This can be handled in five minutes."

"By shaving his head?" Josie cried.

"It won't be the first time," Cameron said with a sigh. "Josie would you mind helping me?"

"Sure," she said, and Alice nodded like it was all settled, and before Josie could even make sense of it all, she was in the bathroom with Cameron, about to shave his head.

They were alone. Really...really alone. She could hear him breathing over the sound of her heart pounding. And she didn't know if she was strong enough to do this. To be close to him like this.

"You don't have to do this," he said, reaching for the clippers. His hand was bigger than she remembered, and he had a fingernail going black from some trauma she wanted to ask him about. "Josie?"

She sucked in a breath at the sound of her name in his voice.

"You okay?" he asked and his voice was light. It was even joking, a little. Like everything that had happened between them hadn't happened, and she realized that was the way to handle this. The two of them just had to pretend none of it... that night, the kiss, his leaving, seven years of silence...none of it happened.

"This really seems like a bad idea," she said, trying to give reason one last shot.

Cameron looked up at her from where he sat on the toilet, a towel around his neck.

"I don't know," he said with that crooked smile. "Seems kind of familiar."

"I messed it up when we were kids, too. Remember the Mohawk fiasco of your senior year?"

"I loved it," he insisted. "I loved it so much."

"No one loves a ratty lopsided Mohawk in their senior pictures." She considered the boy he'd been. "Except you."

"Do it," he said and closed his eyes, head tilted up.

She could kiss him. Just lean down and press her lips to his.

God. This bathroom is so small.

"It's only hair, Josie," he said, opening one eye.

"Right! Of course. It's your head." The whine of the clippers drowned out the opportunity to talk and filled the tiny bathroom with enough noise that it was actually hard to think. She ran the clippers over his head, the pretty silky-brown hair falling down around his shoulders.

She caught some in her hand, trying to keep it out of his eyes.

"Sorry," she whispered, her breath caught in her throat.

"It's okay."

"I just need..." She stepped sideways and he shifted out of her way. Not opening his legs so she could step between them. That, she realized would be...too much. Way too much. As it was, her knee hit his. Her palm skated over his hair, hovering over the shape of his skull.

He breathed out.

She breathed in.

His shoulders gathered hair and she picked it up and threw it in the sink, her fingers registering the warmth of him beneath the towel. Beneath the shirt.

"Can I..."

"I can't hear you."

She turned off the clippers for a second. "I need to clean up around your ears. Can I...touch you?"

"Seems like you already are."

They kept bumping into each other. Elbows. Shoulders. Knees. His thigh. Hers.

She changed the number on the clipper and did her best to dress things up in the back and around his ears. So he didn't look so much like a prisoner of war.

"There," she said and turned off the clippers again. "Look at me."

He did, smiling. And she was distracted by that crooked tooth for just a second.

"That bad?"

"No, actually...I mean, yes. It's pretty terrible. But it's not a lopsided Mohawk."

He stood and she shifted out of his way, but he was so big he filled the tiny powder room. And she stepped back into the doorway to give him the chance to look at himself in the mirror.

It wasn't a great haircut, but it wasn't terrible. It made his eyes bigger and his cheekbones and chin sharper. Stronger. He looked, well, he looked beautiful.

"Not too bad," he said, turning sideways, running his hand over his head. She closed her hand into a fist, wondering if it was actually a bad thing that she knew exactly how his hair felt. "Thank you, Josie."

Their eyes met in the mirror and she couldn't pretend anymore. Everything she wanted to say to him and had swallowed and swallowed and swallowed came pouring out.

"I'm so sorry."

"It's not that bad, Josie!"

"No. That night. For getting you kicked out."

She stopped, the words getting crushed under the silence, thick and heavy between them. "I shouldn't have said anything," she whispered. "I'm sorry." She reached behind her for the door and he reached out and touched her hand, a glancing brush of his fingers against her thumb, and she jerked back. Away. All of her was on edge. Electric.

"You didn't get me kicked out," he said quietly.

"Cameron, please. Please. For the last seven years, whenever your name comes up, everyone suddenly stops being able to look me in the eye. Alice is still mad at me. I tried to explain. I did, but they—"

He stepped forward and the bathroom was the size of a stamp. She could taste him in the air. If her fingers twitched forward they would touch him.

"They didn't kick me out," he said. "I left."

"Because they kicked you out."

He shook his head. And again, she got caught up in the years. The time since she last saw him. A man still carrying his awkward teenage self in his eyes and hands. Who'd become this man standing here now. So solid. So real. And she knew that all of those changes would have happened had they stayed in touch. Had they lived the life she'd fantasized about. He would have grown those shoulders. That beard. The long hair. He would have gotten tall and lean and utterly competent.

But maybe in a different way.

Or maybe, somehow, not at all.

Maybe he would have become some other different version of himself entirely.

Better. Worse. Hard to say.

"I'm so sorry I kissed you."

Impossibly he reached for her and brushed her cheek, and as if that wasn't enough, he cupped her cheek in his hand, his thumb touching the edge of her mouth. She gasped, pulling in air because she was drowning in this little bathroom. Drowning in all the things she hadn't felt with another man. All the things she hadn't felt for years. It was like he touched her and her body came roaring back to life.

"I'm not," he said.

9

JOSIE

She jerked away, unable to bear his touch. It felt like he was laughing at her.

"Don't say that," she said. *Don't say it if it's not true. Don't say it just to make me feel better.*

"What do you remember from that night?" he asked.

Everything and nothing.

"I remember you didn't want to kiss me. You kept trying to get me to stop. I pulled you onto the bed." The memory was excruciating.

"Do you remember what we said?"

"No."

"I wanted to kiss you, Josie. But not like that. Not when you were drunk. I'd been waiting years to kiss you."

"Years?"

He gave her a sideways glance. "Are you going to pretend you didn't know?"

"I'm not pretending anything, Cameron. I spent years nursing an unrequited crush on you. I worked up enough courage and did enough Jell-O shots and kissed you and you vanished." She was getting angry.

"The summer you turned sixteen, remember?"

"What about it?"

"What did we do?"

"You and I ran the 10K race with Jonah in town and then came home for cake and presents."

"After the race, what did you do?"

"Cameron, I don't know what you're talking about."

"They had that rain tent, because it was so hot, and you took off your shirt and went into the rain tent in your shorts and sports bra and you came out..." He stopped, shook his head, his eyes wide like he still couldn't believe it. "I could never look at you the same again. You were sixteen and had been like a sister to me, and suddenly the way I was looking at you was so wrong."

Wrong. She flinched at the word.

Everything she'd felt for him had seemed so right and for him it was *wrong.*

"You were a kid," he said. "And I was an employee, and Max..."

"I get it," she said. Because for Cameron so much of everything came down to Max.

"We were young. But I loved you, too." He'd said *we were young* like it mitigated their feelings. Like their love had been less real instead of more. And maybe that was true for him. In fact, clearly that was true for him.

But that love, that young love, had been the most real thing she'd ever felt.

"I...I didn't know," she said. "I honestly thought it was just me."

They were whispering in the tiny bathroom. That they were standing so close after all these years was actually hard to grasp. She nodded because words were too hard to form.

"I held on to your graduation night," he whispered. "That kiss. The way you felt against my body."

Something was happening. Time was an accordion and folding in on itself. It was now, yes, seven years later, but it was also that night and like not a moment had passed. And her body suddenly came out of the deep freeze where she kept it, woke up and *yearned.*

Watching her the whole time, he cupped the bun at the back of her head in his palm and squeezed, and she gasped at the pleasure–pain of it all. Her head tilted back, her throat bare to him.

But all he did was look at her, his hand clenched in her hair.

It was shocking.

What is happening?

What would I do if he asked? What would I give him?

The answer bubbled up unchanged from the past—anything. Everything.

The clippers nearly slipped out of her numb fingers.

This was too much. Way too much. She stepped back, hitting the toilet. He stepped back, too, bumping into the doorframe.

Her sigh was broken and strained, and she wanted to haul him close and push him away all at the same time. She was torn right down the middle of her extremely uncomfortable desire for the man she'd loved as a boy.

"You should go," she said. *Please go.* "Before Alice comes looking for you. I'll clean this up."

"You sure?" he asked, looking down at the hair in the sink.

"Totally."

She grinned the wide plastic grin her face had grown used to and silently begged him to go, so she could take a deep breath and shake out her hands and remember she wasn't a girl suffering from the most painful case of unrequited love of all time.

But then, suddenly, he grabbed her hand, the one not holding the clippers, and instinctively her hand grabbed back and it seemed—for a moment—that they were holding on to each other. Him in the hallway, her in the tiled bathroom. Both of them in the now and in the past.

"It's good to see you," he said.

"It's good to see you, too."

They were speaking in understatements to somehow make this all seem normal. Or simple. When it was anything but. At least on her end.

Though, maybe it was simple on his end. Maybe he ran into old girlfriends all the time and buried his hands in their hair and pulled, just enough to make them...wet.

She couldn't find the plastic smile so she didn't even look at him.

He squeezed her hand and then walked away.

When she couldn't hear him in the hallway or the dining room she collapsed against the sink.

Hearing his side of the story rearranged things in her head. Alleviated some guilt. Changed the position of the blame and responsibility and left it without any place to go. It didn't take away the pain.

It didn't change that he'd left without a word.

It didn't change that part of her remained caught in that night, in those years with him. Measuring every man against the memory of him. Measuring every man against the way her body had lit up for him.

It was why she hadn't moved on.

It was why she was a twenty-three-year-old virgin.

It was embarrassing. Infuriating. It wasn't his fault that she was frozen. But it wasn't *not* his fault, either. And after that night part of her...shrank. Her confidence, maybe. Her fierceness when it came to her place in this family. She'd taken all that fierceness and put it in her work while her private self stayed small. Withered almost.

It all shuffled in her brain. Some things making more sense. Some things making less.

She understood why he left. Cameron would have been horrified. Embarrassed. He would have felt that he'd betrayed the family.

But it didn't explain the rest of it. Those unreturned calls. Those unread messages. Dozens of them. Hundreds.

She stood staring at a Christmas wreath on a store's door in Greenwich Village. It was one of the green ones, made entirely out of plants. And without thinking twice she called him. His number, six months later, still on her favorites list.

"This is Cameron," his message said. "I probably won't listen to this but go ahead and give it a shot. If you really need me, text."

The sound of his voice put a lump in her throat. And she'd tried texting. She'd tried a bajillion texts.

"Cameron," she said after the beep. "It's...well, it's me. Josie. It's Christmas. Though, you probably know that. I just..." She looked at that wreath, the pine needles and the sage. Someone bumped into her. Slush covered the toes of her boots.

"Move on," someone yelled at her and she laughed. Exactly. Move on.

"Wanted to wish you a Merry Christmas. I hope you're well. Call...you know...if you want to."

He'd never called and she wished she could say that was the last time she'd called him. He hadn't returned one of her texts and now he stood there and had the gall to tell her he had felt what she had felt.

Bullshit.

She was stunned to feel...anger. Real anger. It exploded in her. Out of the boxes where she'd put it. Where she'd *hidden* it.

Leaving the clippers and the hair, she went to get some answers.

10

————

CAMERON

His hand burned. He flexed it, spreading the fingers wide, and then clenched it into a fist. He could feel every strand of her hair that he'd touched.

What was that? he wondered.

Well, he knew what that was. That thing between them that made her breath break and her eyes dilate. That made his blood burn. It was what had always been between them. And what a goddamn kick in the nuts that he'd never felt that same burn with any other woman. That same chemistry.

In Thailand he'd met Paanit, a chef who worked out of a beach cave, and Paanit served him spicy Khao soi and grilled meat from a smoky fire with an oily, bright-green condiment he'd never had before. It was so delicious, the perfect combination of sweet and salt and heat with bright herbaceous tones, that it had blown his mind. Paanit, the bastard, wouldn't tell him what was in it and Cameron had spent years trying to recreate the taste.

He'd come close, but finally had to admit that the difference between what he could make and what Paanit had made for him was the magic that came from the experience and the person making it.

This powerful desire he felt for Josie was exactly like that. He'd spent years trying to feel for another woman what he felt for that girl he met when they were both too young.

And never came close.

His bag was at the base of the steps and he stopped beside it. How easy it would be to leave. He wanted to leave because there was no way to keep things separate with her. To keep it clean. Neat. His desire for her was a desire not just for her body—but for all of her. Her secrets and their past, who they'd been. If he stayed—with her—things were gonna get messy.

"Cameron!"

He whirled at the sound of her voice, the furious stomp of her feet.

Brace yourself, he thought. But what exactly he was bracing himself for he wasn't sure. The sight of her, her red hair slipping out of that bun, falling in fat curls over her shoulders - her eyes narrowed, her cheeks pink -- it lit him up.

Oh, he thought. *She's so fucking amazing when she's mad.*

"I called you every day," she said, coming to a stop a foot from him. He could see the pound of her heart right there in the fragile skin of her neck.

"For a month. I know."

"I emailed. I messaged."

"Everyone did." He tried to smile. But she was not having it.

She shook her head. "Why? Why couldn't you answer the phone? Send one text? One message from you and..."

"What?" he asked. "One message from me and what?"

"I would have moved on."

"No." He stepped forward, narrowing the distance between them. "One message from me and then it would have been another one. And then another. And then I'd call you some night from a hostel in who the hell knows where and you'd call me from New York and then we'd never move on. Never. I needed to cut all ties, Josie."

She opened her mouth as if to blast him again, but Alice came shouting through the door from the kitchen.

"Cameron! Oh." She lowered her voice. "There you are."

He turned away from Josie, broke that connection between them, and sucked in a breath.

"Everything okay?" Alice asked, looking between them.

"Fine," Josie snapped, and he nearly smiled. The woman with the fake smile and the eyes full of tears, those weren't versions of Josie he was familiar with. But this version, angry and spitting fire...yeah, he knew that girl.

He *loved* that girl.

"I've got the focaccia dough rising," Alice said.

"You want me to start assembling the lasagnas?" he asked, walking forward, eagerly ready to get away from this girl who made his skin burn and spine tingle. And made him *remember*...

"We've got some time," Alice said. "But I need to run into town to Knapstein's to get the turkeys and roast."

"I'll go," he said.

Alice blinked. "Well, Mateo would love to see you." She tossed the truck keys she had in her hand, and Cameron snagged them out of the air.

"And I'd love to see him."

"You might..." Alice looked over his shoulder at Josie. "Need some help."

"Absolutely," Josie said, enunciating every part of that

word. And he could feel her dark-eyed gaze like knives at his back.

"What about work?" he asked her, turning back around.

"It can wait."

Alice made some kind of strangled, surprised laughing sound but swallowed it quickly.

"Let's go," Josie said.

THE OLD TRUCK smelled like a thousand school lunches and something else on top of it. Something funky.

"What is that smell?" he asked.

"Dom's hockey stuff. Apparently, Max uses the truck to take him back and forth to practice."

"Oh god, I've never been so glad not to play hockey," he joked. She didn't laugh.

Their breath made smoky plumes in the cold air of the truck. "I see the heater is still top notch," he said, cranking the thing as high as it could go. Half the time the truck wouldn't be warm until you got to you destination. "I can't believe it's still running," he said to her silence, because he was a rambling fool at the moment. He put the truck in Drive and they were off down the road. Josie buckled into the passenger seat with her pink cheeks and the red knit hat she'd pulled on over her hair.

She was prickly with anger, and the perverse thing about him was...he liked it.

Sexual tension sat on the bench seat between them. Where it had waited since she turned sixteen and he could no longer pretend she was just some little kid following him around.

"Do you remember where to go?" she asked.

He nodded. Knapstein's was the butcher in Athens

who'd managed to survive all those years when no one went to a neighborhood butcher anymore, and instead picked up their meat in big cellophane-wrapped packages from Costco and marveled at the value without knowing— really—what they were eating.

Now the world wanted a bespoke butcher experience. And Mateo, like his father and his grandfather and his great-grandfather before him, was there to provide it. "Do you?" he asked. "Alice said you haven't been back in five years."

He glanced over to see her lift her chin, her eyes on the road ahead of them.

"I remember," she said. In the tone that said, *I remember everything.* And the problem was, so did he. And the tension in the truck was almost too much. And it wasn't just the sexual tension or all the questions they were afraid to ask or the answers they were afraid to hear. He wanted to roll down the window just to breathe.

"Why?" she asked, popping the tension. "Why didn't you ever pick up the phone? Just to let me know you were okay."

They were doing this. Really doing it.

"I was mad."

"At me?"

"No. God no. At Max. Alice. Myself, mostly."

"Why?"

Oh god. He really didn't want to talk about this. Bringing it up made it real. Made it *now*. And he liked all this stuff in the past.

"Because I'd waited a year, Josie, to tell you how I felt, and I let the whole night get away from me. I was sober. And older. It should have happened another way."

She opened her mouth and he knew she was going to

apologize again. And he didn't need her being more sorry for something that he didn't blame her for.

"And I was embarrassed," he said before she could say anything. "And proud. And being a martyr." He managed to smile at her very serious face, her auburn hair poking out from under that hat in the most endearing way. "I knew you would get over me."

"You knew that, did you?"

"You were young, Jose. And beautiful and about to start school in New York. You had everything ahead of you. When I think about it now, it was ridiculous to think there was even a chance the two of us could work."

He stopped, waiting, maybe, for her to argue. He wasn't sure. But she turned her face away, looking out the window. And her silence said plenty. It had been ridiculous to think that what they'd felt for each other would have survived. He'd been a sixteen-year-old kid inside a twenty-two-year-old body. He'd known nothing of the world or himself. And she'd been about to set the world on fire.

"And then it was just easier to move on. To forget."

"Did you?" she asked.

"Sometimes," he said. "Sometimes I wouldn't think about the Riverview for days."

And other days it was all I could think about.

"And you must have," he said.

"Must have what?"

"Moved on. Alice said you haven't been back in five years."

"Work," she said, looking down at her hands, the red mittens they'd found in the closet to match the hat, because all her winter stuff was at Max and Delia's. "It's...all-consuming."

"See? Clearly it was for the best. I mean, look at you, Josie. Look at what you've done. You're so accomplished."

He was trying to push them out of the past and into the present. The present he could talk about.

Come on, he thought. *Let it go. Let who we were and what we were to each other go. Let that night go.*

The tension between them pulled taut again, like she was wrapping her feelings around her fists, ready for a fight. But there was nothing to fight about. They were both okay. It had all been for the best. Surely, she had to see that.

And then she took a deep breath, and just like that the tension slipped away.

"I don't know, you're kind of a big deal, Cameron," she finally said with a big smile and he sighed with relief. The muscles of his body loosened.

"Yes, in primitive cooking circles, I am a very big deal." He smiled, the king of self-deprecation.

"All those chefs you've gotten to lure out of their kitchens to your campfire..."

"Well, once Jamie Oliver did it, it wasn't hard to convince lots of them to try it."

"Stop downplaying what you've done. You always did that," she said. "Made your accomplishments seem like accidents when I know how hard you had to work for everything."

He blinked.

"Funny," he whispered. "You sound exactly the same as you did when we were kids."

"Bossy?" she asked with a laugh. "Because I've kind of made a career out of it."

"Yes. But I also never had a cheerleader quite like you."

Yeah. He wasn't so good at staying out of the past. Not with her. In every other part of his life, his childhood and his time at the inn were in a shoebox he could shove into some far closet corner. But with her, well...the past was very much part of his present.

He pulled the truck into town. A one-road stretch leading down to the Hudson, lined with shops and restaurants and bars. The street was dressed up in its very best Christmas clothes. Lights and greenery wrapped around the black cast-iron light posts. Wreaths were on every doorway. The shops selling last-minute stocking-stuffers and the restaurants offering lunches to those last-minute stocking-stuffer shoppers were doing a brisk business.

There was a fancy olive oil shop and a cheese shop. A shop that just sold...he couldn't even tell. Lawn ornaments?

"Wow," Josie murmured. "It looks great, doesn't it?"

"Yeah," he said. "It's really changed in the last few years. It's..." He struggled to find the word.

"Posh?"

"This was Gabe's dream," Cameron said. "He wanted the inn to be the kind of place that would raise the tide for the whole town. All the businesses."

The main strip used to be dive bars and tattoo parlors. A shuttered shoe shop. The tattoo parlor was still there, but even it had been shined up. And he hadn't realized until this moment that he'd spent most of his life planning on being there to see all this happen. And he didn't regret the direction his life had taken, but he wished he could have watched the transformation.

Maybe...maybe I shouldn't have stayed away. But that was a double-edged sword. If he hadn't stayed away, he wouldn't have made his life what it was. And there was no point in regret. Or what-ifs. That wasn't how he lived. And staying away had been the only way to avoid get sucked back into this place. These people.

He was all about the clean breaks. The simple goodbyes. If you never loved anyone, leaving was easy.

"You okay?" she asked and he could sense her about to put a hand on his shoulder. And he dodged that bullet by popping open the door, letting the cold air swirl in and banish the warmth.

"Let's go."

11

JOSIE

She shouldn't have come. She'd gotten angry and righteous and she'd made a decision without thinking it through. And now she had all the answers she didn't really want.

It was for the best.

It was ridiculous to think we could be anything.

You got over me.

No, she wanted to say. She hadn't. She hadn't gotten over him one bit.

But he had so clearly gotten over her that she kept her mouth shut.

This is a good thing, she told herself as she followed Cameron into the butcher shop. *You got the answers you didn't know you needed and now you can move on. Yay.*

The bell tinkled over the door as Cameron and Josie stepped inside.

Knapstein's, much like the downtown street, had had a face-lift. It had always been pretty, with original wood floors and ceilings, but the last time she'd been in there the place had shown its age, which was over a hundred years. Mateo, the fourth generation Knapstein to take over the butcher shop, had given it some new life.

Dark-stained wooden floors and ceiling. Chalkboard paint on one wall with specials and prices. Staff were serving customers from gleaming stainless-steel cold cases and wearing smart denim aprons with the old-fashioned logo embroidered on the front.

Christmas music played in the background. And the air smelled of roasted chicken and potatoes.

Mateo's mother, Nancy, was a Portuguese woman his father had met while on vacation, and their marriage had brought new energy to the store. Mateo, it would seem, was running with it.

"My god!" Mateo said from the far counter. He used the back of his wrist to push his glasses up high on his nose. "Is that Five Questions Cameron?"

"Mateo," Cameron said, smiling. "Look at what you've done to this place."

Mateo, his dark, bald head gleaming under the warm lights, came out from behind the counter, and he and Cameron hugged with much backslapping and smiling. Mateo was several years older than Cameron, but since the inn got all their meat from Knapstein's, the two had formed a strong friendship.

Had he just walked away from Mateo, too?

"I got your email," Mateo said. "Sorry I haven't had a chance to respond. It's been nuts with the holiday."

I guess not.

"Look at this place," Cameron said, taking it all in. "Your parents would be so proud."

Mateo smiled, his arm still around Cameron. "Thanks,

man. Though they'd have an opinion on everything I'm changing."

"That's for sure," Cameron said and then stepped back to include Josie in their circle. "You remember Josie? Max and Delia's daughter."

"Of course. The runner. Good to see you. You're here picking up Alice's order?"

"We are," Josie said. "And this place is gorgeous."

"Thank you, thank you," Mateo said. "We've gotten into some prepared foods. Churrasaco." He pointed to the display case with the Portuguese roasted chickens in their crispy skins. The potatoes and rice. "Sauces and marinades." He was pointing at the jars on shelves. The freezer cases full of shepherd's pie and Bolognese sauce. Jars of pickles. Spice blends and piri-piri sauce, chimichurri, all his mother's recipes. Which had been her grandmother's recipes.

It was all the perfect combination of the old and the new.

Inspiration struck.

"You should do five questions with Mateo," she said, and both Cameron and the butcher turned to look at her. Internally, she winced. It was hard to turn off the good television filter. "Fifth generation butcher? Mom's traditional recipes?" She shrugged. "Seems like a good one to me."

Cameron blinked at her and then smiled so wide, that crooked tooth was revealed. She glanced away to read the price of ground beef per pound, her hand to her stomach, which had twisted in the face of that smile.

"What do you say, Mateo?" Cameron asked.

"Come on," Mateo said, wiping a hand across his shiny head. "No one's going to care what I've got to say."

"I don't know," Cameron said. "I think the television producer might be on to something."

"Okay," Mateo finally said, still seeming nervous. But the endearing kind of nervous. Excited and pleased to be asked. "Right now?"

"No, you're busy," Cameron looked around at the customers, who were watching them.

"Nah, my kids got it." Mateo pointed over to the thin young men helping other customers. They looked like teenagers.

"You are too young to have kids that old." Cameron said.

"Well, me and Mich started young. When you know what you want, why wait? So?" he asked. "You want to go in back? The lighting is good, but it's not as pretty."

"Right there," Josie said and pointed over at the old butcher block that stood between two cold cases. It was the block Mateo's great-grandfather had used to cut up the cows and sheep and goats that area farmers would bring him.

Cameron gave her a look she couldn't read. "Sorry," she said. "I'll keep my mouth shut."

Cameron and Mateo started to set up.

Adjust that light, she thought just as Cameron reached over and tilted a wall sconce slightly away from Mateo so the light wouldn't reflect off his glasses. *Ask him about the butcher block*, she thought, just as she heard Cameron say, "I'm going to ask you about your great-grandfather's butcher block. Tell me the whole story. Don't be your usual modest self."

"I'll try to get my brag on," Mateo joked, looking handsome and serious.

This was going to be a good one. The best part, and she wondered if Cameron had figured it out, was that until now he hadn't interviewed anyone who knew him very well. There had been some female guests who gave the impression that they were *going* to get to know Cameron real well once the camera was off. But no one like Mateo.

And then Cameron and Mateo started, and they were joking and telling old stories, and the sound of their laughter pulled everyone's eyes to them. Where they stayed for twenty minutes.

"Can I help you?" One of Mateo's sons asked.

When you know what you want, why wait?

Funny how that advice could backfire.

"I'm here for the Riverview Inn order," she said.

A HALF HOUR LATER, after Cameron and Josie made promises to stop in at Mateo's annual Boxing Day open house at his place by the river, they finally got back out to the truck where Josie had already loaded the turkeys and roasts, the specially cut bacon and the smoked ham.

"I didn't think you would be sticking around for Boxing Day," she said. "And since when did everyone around here start celebrating it?"

"Since it extended the holiday," Cameron said. "Alice got the British Christmas vibe and was able to charge top price for eggs."

"Come on, really?"

"You know Alice, always looking for a way to make something special."

"And cost more," she said. "But you're sticking around? For the day after Christmas?"

"My plans are loose. And we're going to do some butchering for the second part of his episode. It's worth sticking around for. But what about you? Don't you have to get back to the city?"

She entertained the thought of actually going to that

open house with Cameron. They'd take a bottle of wine; he'd put his hand at the small of her back while they talked to people. She'd laugh at his jokes. It would be like an alternate reality. Who they would have been if that night hadn't happened. "I do," she said. "I'm leaving Christmas morning."

"That was a really good interview," Cameron said as he started the truck.

"You're a good interviewer." She pushed the vents to blast their bodies with warm air. The sun had gone down while they were in the shop and the temperatures had dropped hard. They'd had a long, laughing argument over the best cut of steak and how Mateo's father had taught him to butcher a pig when he was ten. It had been a somewhat bloody conversation.

"It didn't occur to me to ask him. That was all you."

"Cameron," she said. "I do know something about reality television."

"Congrats on the new job," he said, glancing sideways at her. "Executive producer."

"How do you know about that?' she asked, and all at once she felt every barrier that had been abandoned the last few hours rise back up, ready to protect something she didn't want to talk about. Protect something, even though she didn't totally understand why she was protecting it.

"I have been known to cyber stalk you," he confessed.

"Well, I suppose that's fair. I have been known to binge your YouTube videos."

"That's how you knew Mateo would be good."

"You have a real ability to click with people. You do a pretty good job of faking it when you don't have chemistry with a guest—which is rare," she said. Because Cameron could create a connection with a couch. "But when it's real, it's really fun to watch." There were some things he could do to increase his chances of making a connection. Pre-planning and pre-interview stuff. But his was a bare-bones operation. She got that. His empathy and curiosity were enough to get him through.

"I don't...I don't know what to say to that." He sounded like he didn't often get compliments. Which was bullshit; the guy was a success, people had to be coming out of the woodwork to praise him.

"There's nothing to say." She shrugged. "It's a statement of fact."

"How about you? How was your work emergency this morning?"

She opened her mouth and then shut it. Opened it again, shut it again.

CAMERON

Tell me, he thought. *Please. Tell me.*

It was astonishing how much he wanted her to tell him what was bothering her. How much he wanted to be let into her life. To occupy that space with her—to be someone's confidant. Friend. Amazing how much he missed that.

And he'd never really realized it until right now. Until being back with her in this damn truck.

Finally, she blurted, "Meaningless. My job really only has meaningless emergencies."

She shut her mouth again, like she hadn't meant to tell the truth.

"Meaningless?" he repeated, and she shot him a sideways glance.

"Nice try."

"What?"

"I remember you told me how all the counselors and therapists you went to when you were a kid tried to get you to open up."

"I did?" Of course he had. He'd told her all his secrets. The teenage Cameron had been a real blabbermouth.

"Repeat the most important word in the sentence, but like it's a question."

"Question?" he asked.

"Stop!" she cried, and he finally smiled. "It's...you know, a little telling that you thought the most important word in my sentence was *meaningless*."

The heater was doing enough of its job that she pulled off her mittens and worried the wrist of one of them with her fingers.

"I'm trying to change things," she said and then shook her head like she hadn't been planning on saying that. "Make the show into something else. Something we could all be proud of."

"And?"

"They're reviewing my pitch," she said, smiling a little. And he could tell she was hedging her bets. "But signs look good. It would be for next year."

"What's your pitch?" he asked.

"It doesn't...you can't be that interested."

He was interested in everything about her. "Of course I am. Lay it on me."

She explained her idea of putting people with different ideas and philosophies and religions and backgrounds in a series of booths so they couldn't see each other, and instead of answering questions about what made them different, they had to answer questions about what made them similar.

"Things like their favorite food their mother made, the

name of their first pet, what they did on summer vacation when they were young. What they wanted to be when they grew up. Things they're scared of, things like that."

"So they talk about what they have in common, rather than what they stand in opposition to."

"Yeah," she said. "I feel like we're all so divided."

"You're assuming people have the same kind of childhood," he said. And he could feel her focus. "I didn't have a pet. My mom didn't make me food I loved."

"You're right. I've thought about this, but I'm not sure how to resolve the issue. Except maybe to just let it be an issue. Maybe that is how we open people's eyes to how privilege works."

"That's a lot to ask of reality television. It's really ambitious."

"I think there's room to ask more of television. We've sunk down to the lowest common denominator. I think we can ask more of television and more of our viewers."

"That's the Josie I remember," he said with a smile.

"I'm calling it *Common Ground*. And maybe it is too ambitious or big, but I'm ready for something exciting, even if it means making it on my own."

"Josie," he said and then didn't know what else to say. Or how to put what he felt about her into words. "It's a complicated, amazing idea."

You're amazing.

"I feel like your show manages to bring people of different backgrounds together over food and coffee," she said.

"I don't have a show."

"Come on, Five Questions is totally a show. You have, like, a million subscribers, Cameron."

"I really don't know how that happened."

"Oh my god, that you somehow stumbled into YouTube success is the most Cameron thing I've ever heard."

She was smiling at him and he was smiling at her, and for a moment, bright and hot, it was like every moment since she kissed him on her graduation night to now had never happened. And those things that had happened to the two of them over the course of living their lives had been shared.

She wasn't a stranger. She was his best friend. Had been. Back when he'd had that kind of thing.

And he didn't look away. And she didn't, either. And his longing for her, for what they might have been, was painful. Excruciating.

"You've really made a name for yourself," she said quietly into the loaded air.

"That's what I'm told."

"You know something?" She laughed. "Fuck that."

"What?"

"Yeah, fuck that *oh I just stumbled onto something* and *I'm just lucky* and *I'm not paying attention to the money.*"

"What are you talking about?" He laughed.

"You don't have all those followers without paying attention." He glanced over at her and she raised an eyebrow. "I'm just saying you can cut the act. With me. You can be honest. I know exactly what that kind of success takes and how hard you have to work to keep it."

With me. You can be honest.

"So?" She knew the drill. The energy around these self-made stars and everyone trying to capitalize on it.

"YouTube and Netflix keep calling me in for meetings," he said.

"They want to do a show?" she asked

"Yeah."

"And you?"

"I like what I'm doing."

Her silence was telling. So was the way she was staring at him. "What?" he asked with a laugh.

"What what?" She shrugged one shoulder.

"You want to say something and you're stopping yourself."

"I don't..." The coyness fell away for a moment. "I don't know you well enough to tell you your business—"

He put a hand out, stretched it across the back of the seat and touched her shoulder. Just slipped his hand over her coat, and he could only feel the shape of her beneath that coat.

She shifted and his fingers, icy cold, touched the hot skin of her neck and they both gasped.

He pulled away, put both hands back around the steering wheel.

"You knew me better than anyone else." He shrugged.

"That was a long time ago," she said.

"Was it?" He glanced over at her. "Because it doesn't feel like it. Not tonight."

What the hell are you doing? This whole conversation felt like it was tempting fate in a way fate did not need to be tempted. The past was the past.

"Being back," he said into the quiet truck. "I can still feel that teenager I was when I first got here." He pressed his hand against his chest as if showing her where that kid was hiding out.

"You mean Chaz?" she joked. It was the name he tried to get everyone to call him for about five minutes when he first arrived. Max had put the kibosh on that real quick.

"Yeah, him." Her grin was bright white in the gloom of the twilight. "All that posturing. All that fear. How badly I wanted Alice and Max to..." He stopped and whistled. But the words he was going to say hung in the air as clearly as if he'd shouted them.

Love me. Be proud of me.

"Anyway, I used to be so embarrassed by that kid but now...I'm almost fond of him."

"I was pretty fond of him, too," she said. But she looked out the window instead of meeting his gaze. "It's true for me, as well. I mean, it feels like part of me is still that girl. And maybe that's just how people feel when they get older. Like they keep adding to the person they were, piling versions of themselves on top of each other."

"Like those Russian nesting dolls?"

"Yeah. I mean, I can still feel that scared little girl who first arrived here, so angry at her mom. So worried about her dad. Confused about everything. She's still..." She put a hand to her neck. "Here. Her voice still comes out of me."

"You had a pretty traumatic event," he said. "With your dad."

"Thank god for therapy," she joked but he didn't laugh. They were getting closer to the inn, the glow of the main lodge visible over the trees.

Thank god.

"I think about my dad sometimes." Her voice was barely above a whisper. "About the kind of man he was and what parts of him are in me."

"Josie," he said. "You're nothing like your father."

"Well, I'm not a murderer." Again she tried to make things light but Cameron was not having it. He knew how she was trying to deflect. "But I have his height. And his skeptic's nature."

"Stop," he said as they pulled into the back driveway. The truck bounced over the snow and potholes, and the inn, even from the rear, was so pretty. He'd forgotten how pretty it was. Particularly this time of year.

"And he was a person who tore things apart, you know? He loved destruction. It made him feel strong and in control. And sometimes I'm scared that I have that part of him, too."

He slammed the truck into Park and then, shockingly, he grabbed her hands where they were clenched in her lap. His skin was warm, his palms rough with calluses. And then, maybe because she didn't pull back, he touched her face, her cheek, the edge of her lips.

Her lips parted on a broken breath and his thumb touched the damp of her mouth and it was so fucking exciting he couldn't stand it. It was too much and not nearly enough.

"You built me up," he said. "Knowing you gave me the confidence to do everything I've done. You are a builder. Like Max. Your mom. And I can't thank you—"

"Cameron," she whispered, shaking her head.

"Let me thank you, Josie. Please."

"Look at what I did to you. That night—"

"I owe my life to you and to that scared girl who befriended that scared boy so full of attitude. I do. It's a fact. That night didn't change that. And it made what happened next possible."

The words *I love you* almost slipped out. Because he did love her, like the dearest friend he had. But the words were loaded between them. Dipped in other feelings, complicated by what might have been.

A kiss hung in the air. The possibility of *them*. He wanted her with something close to pain. An ache.

"I'm sorry," she whispered and got out of the truck.

12

––––––––

CAMERON

Look. Sex was easy. Sex was the easiest thing in the world. Sex, in Cameron's purview, was always the end. The goodbye. It was the *thank you and take care* between two people. It was the exclamation point on an evening of flirtation. A weekend of banter. Not that he didn't take it seriously. He did. Of course he did. But sex made everything simple. Biological. It left out the brain and it left out the heart.

The brain and the heart were where things got messy.

And everything with Josie was messy and the last thing he needed was to think about sleeping with her. And it was all he could think about.

He watched her that night with the family as they ate dinner. He watched her laugh with Helen and tease her brother about his hair. She and Delia sat back with glasses of red wine and talked, the Christmas tree lights reflected in their hair and eyes.

What a shock to realize he still wanted her. He'd chalked up all the feelings he'd had for her to boyhood. To young love and constant proximity. But a day alone with her in that truck and he was feeling it all again. But sharper. Fiercer.

The breaking of her breath when he pulled her hair in the bathroom. It would have been so easy to tug her closer by that bun. Against his body. He could have shut the door and pushed her against that sink. Or at any point today he could have pulled that truck over on the side of the road and kissed her in all the ways his teenage self had dreamed of.

That list was in his head, the carefully crafted list with all the places on her body he wanted to touch and kiss and *bite.*

Yep.

Maybe this was how they could have the goodbye they should have had. Without the shame. Without the anger. And all the years of silence. Maybe this was a way to rewrite their ending.

It had a kind of poetry to it. A do-over in the best possible way.

And it had the added benefit of putting everything in order. His feelings. His thoughts about what she'd said in the truck about being a person who tore things down rather than building them up.

He didn't understand how she could be so wrong about herself.

"They make a pretty sight, don't they?" Max asked Cameron as he cleared dishes from the table. He and Alice had served Mateo's smoked ham with green beans and Alice's legendary Gratin Dauphinoise.

Cameron felt himself blush, uncomfortable to be caught by Max staring at Josie with these thoughts in his head.

"Hey," Max said, his hands full of dishes. "You want to give me a hand in the kitchen?"

Yeah, Cameron was no dummy. He knew what waited

for him in that kitchen, and there was no way he was going in there for a heart-to-heart.

"I'm not your employee anymore," he said, as cold as he could be, and he got up to join Helen by the fire.

THE NEXT MORNING was much the same as the day before had been.

The smell of coffee pulled him from his bed and down into the kitchen with Alice. Who greeted him with a smile, a mug, and a list of things they had to do.

"We're supposed to get a storm later today," she said, looking out the windows at the low sky.

"Then we better get moving," he said.

They began to assemble the lasagnas and pulled the focaccia out of the fridge where it had been kept for its second rise. The cold kept the rise slow and created a better flavor.

"Hey," Alice said. "I want another shot at Five Questions."

He thought of what Josie'd said about him and people with whom he had chemistry. "Yeah?"

"Yeah. So when can we do it?"

"Well, we're a little busy right now," he said, hedging.

"I won't bring up your mom," she said, and he glanced up at her. She looked as contrite as Alice ever looked. "I'm sorry I did last time."

"No," he said. "It's okay. I mean...it just surprised me is all."

"We can pretend like we don't even know each other," Alice said in a cheery voice that made his soul cringe. "We can—"

"Alice," he said quietly, needing to put a stop to her so

cheerfully vowing to pretend she wasn't the person who'd put him on this path with food. "Let me just...think about it."

"Sure," she said, her voice in some strange octave. "Let me know."

They worked in awkward silence until the back door flew open and there was Josie, wild-eyed and wrapped in cables, holding her laptop.

Her phone was pressed to her ear and she waved at Alice and Cameron as she walked through the kitchen to the living room. "Yeah," she said. "That sounds fine. But does it have to...okay. But if the optics are bad, isn't it just bad? Like, can't we try for good optics? Fine. Yes."

The door closed behind her, and he and Alice shared a knowing look.

"That girl is wasting herself on that stupid show," Alice said.

Cameron tended to agree, but kept his mouth shut. He thought of her new idea and he hoped it would happen. She deserved to be proud of her work.

"She helped me do a Five Questions with Mateo yesterday."

"Mateo gets five questions and I don't?" Alice cried.

"I'm thinking about it," he said with a laugh.

"Was it nice? Working with her?" Alice asked, spreading ricotta mixture over the noodles in the silver pan in front of her.

"Different," he said. "I mean, working with anyone would be different, but she's so smart, you know? And insightful."

Alice nodded and the conversation faded because she wasn't going to push and he wasn't going to say anything else.

Three hours later the foil-wrapped bread and pans of lasagna had been loaded into the back of the van. The bread was still warm from the oven and he could feel it through his gloves. Smell the garlic and basil and tomatoes through the wrap. His stomach growled despite his having just eaten a giant slab of lasagna for lunch.

But he'd reverted to his teenage self here at the Riverview—he was hungry. Hungry for food and for the girl he never got to have.

He'd spent the last three hours looking for reasons to go out into the living room to see her. Talk to her. He took her coffee and fresh focaccia. A piece of lasagna for lunch. And each time he'd gone out, there she'd been, on the phone, but her eyes were warm with thanks and...awareness.

It buzzed between them.

And having her now felt inevitable.

It was the most logical thing. And the idea made his blood leap and his dick hard, and there was a kind of righteous symmetry to the whole thing.

They would have sex and say goodbye to the kids they'd been.

It was enough to make a guy smile.

She was not, he could tell, opposed to the idea. He'd learned a thing or two away from the Riverview. And he knew when a woman was interested in him as a man. And every time he got close to her—setting the coffee cup down, his fingers brushing hers when he handed her the focaccia —her interest practically sparkled and fizzed in the air.

Yeah. As plans went, he liked it.

With the van full of the food for Haven House he went back into the kitchen, where Alice was finishing up the dishes. "You got everything?" she asked.

"Yep."

"You sure you don't want help?"

Oh, I want help. Just not yours.

"I'm good," he said. He left the kitchen and went back to the dining room and the chair and table where Josie had set up camp. Working, it seemed, nonstop. Empty cups of coffee. A plate with smears of lasagna left on it. She'd put on glasses, those big, thick black ones that a certain kind of woman wore.

That certain kind of woman—bookish and serious—was his catnip.

The tree was on, the fire was lit, and she looked like a Christmas angel sitting there.

"Hey," he said, coming up on her side.

"Hey," she said with a careful smile.

"Can you take a break?"

She looked at him like she'd never heard those words before.

"All right. You clearly need a break." He picked up the laptop that she used as a barricade and set it aside. "Let's take a ride."

If there was a person on this planet who needed to relax, it was his old friend. She was wound tight and holding herself so still and so carefully she was about to crack.

Did she know that? he wondered. Could she feel it under her skin, the way her sharp edges were grinding together?

"Where are you going?" she asked.

"Alice needs me to deliver the lasagna down to Haven House," he said.

"Times have not changed, have they?"

"Not at the Riverview. Not with Alice." Make the food and deliver the food had been a way of life for him at the inn when he and Helen and Josie were organizing the lunch program at the elementary school. That felt like a lifetime ago.

"You want to come with me?" he asked.

From her half-shut laptop came a chorus of muffled chimes announcing messages and emails. The never-ending pressure of her job.

Say yes, he thought. But she was silent.

Clearly, the weight of that laptop was heavier than the temptation of what might happen between them.

"Of course," he said, stepping back and waving his hand like he could erase the invitation. "You're busy. I was already interrupting."

"No," she said, and practically jumped to her feet. She fully shut the laptop so it wasn't binging at her, but picked up her phone and slipped it into her back pocket. So, not totally untethered. "I'd love to help."

"Well, full disclosure, Alice said if we showed up down there Daphne and Jonah would put us to work wrapping presents."

"Oh my god, remember that year we had to wrap all the presents for the Haven House families? We were there until four a.m."

He took a deep breath and nodded. "I remember all the years, Josie. All of them."

IN THE TRUCK Josie sat as far from him as she could, practically leaning into the passenger-side door. "So? Tell me the truth about Netflix and your YouTube channel."

He turned onto the road leading toward the highway down the mountain to Athens Organics and Haven House.

He liked that she watched his show. Maybe more than he should. For a guy with a million followers, he always—

every single time he uploaded a video—wondered if one of those million was her. And he'd wanted it to be. Ached for it to be.

"The truth about the show," he said, "is that I've had some luck. And every once in a while, I have a few good ideas. And then...some more luck." He shrugged.

"Do you like it?"

"I like cooking and talking about food and learning about food. But the bullshit around a *show*..."

"Yeah, that's not really your style."

"Not even a little bit. But it's kind of a machine at this point. It runs itself. I mean, I don't mind the idea of branching out and trying new things. But what Netflix and YouTube want from me doesn't feel like *me*." Big fat flakes of snow started to twirl down from the gray sky overhead. The beginning of the storm they were supposed to get.

"What about your job?" he asked. "Whole lot more glamorous than making coffee on some mountainside."

"Nothing about what I'm doing is glamorous. Or even interesting." She sighed.

"Then quit."

She laughed.

"I'm serious."

"And do what?"

"Literally anything. You can do literally anything, Josie. Take Common Ground someplace else."

She rolled her head across the window.

"You used to say that to me all the time," he said. "The night of your graduation you said it, and it was like I heard you. And I believed that you believed it, but I just could never believe it myself. And if I hadn't left this place...I might not have ever believed it."

"You're saying quit my job and belief will come?"

"Yep."

"Said by the guy who doesn't have to pay rent in Queens."

He laughed. "True, but so is what I'm saying. Sometimes you have to let go of one thing to grab onto another."

"It's not that simple."

"Yeah, it is. You just don't want it to be." She was silent and he glanced over to see if she was glaring at him, but she was looking out the window, chewing on her lip. A classic Josie tell that she was thinking deep thoughts.

"Hey," he said. "Alice wants to do a Five Questions."

"That's a great idea," she said. "I'm surprised you haven't done it yet."

"Well, I started one yesterday but she brought up my mom and I stopped. And she said today that we could try again and she'd pretend she didn't know me."

"That would be awful," Josie said.

"For her?"

"No. Awful TV."

"What should I do?" he asked.

"Oh, I think you know what you should do," she said. "You should do a Five Questions with her all about your relationship. And how you came to be at the inn and what she taught you and what you learned from her. It should be a total reveal about your beginning in the kitchen."

"No one wants to see that," he said.

"Everyone wants to see that. And you should be peeling potatoes while you do it."

"You make it sound easy," he said.

"It is. You just don't want it to be." She smiled at him like it was nothing how coy she was being. So coy he wanted to pull this truck over and get his hands under her shirt, teach her a lesson about what happened to girls who smiled like that.

God, the things I want to do to you.

He turned from the road onto the winding driveway that led to Athens Organics and Haven House.

"Wow, it's gotten a lot bigger," he said as they pulled up to park in front of the farmhouse.

He had a painful déjà vu. The last time he was here had been the night of Josie's graduation. Helen had had a fake ID and sneaked out of the house to join Josie at the parties, but then got drunk and called her mom to tell her she loved her. Classic Helen.

He felt all the years, all at once. The years he'd been here. And the years he was away.

Part of him had believed that the inn and the farm and Haven House would sort of hang in suspended animation. Unchanging. And he was glad there had been progress, of course he was glad, it was just strange not to have seen it. Not to have helped.

Yeah. That was it. There'd been a lot of changes he hadn't been a part of.

When, for a lot of years, all he'd wanted was to help this place grow.

There was a giant greenhouse behind the farm now. Daphne was experimenting with hydroponics. And one of the sheds he knew was devoted to her mushrooms. Behind and beside the greenhouses, the fields were all sleeping under the snow. The orchard, too. Next door was Haven House, built when he still lived at the farm. He'd had one summer job helping the contractor clear the area. He'd gotten poison ivy so badly he'd blown up like a balloon.

Don't you know what poison ivy looks like? Josie had asked, rubbing calamine lotion on his arms.

I do now, he'd said, the excruciating embarrassment giving the itch a run for its money.

Haven House looked like a cross between a stately manor home and a very beautiful hotel. There were porches and balconies outside every window. White gingerbread nestled into peaked roofs. And all of it right now was covered in Christmas lights. Some blinking and flashing. Some steady and plain white. It was like a patchwork quilt of lights. Daphne's doing. She didn't like uniformity or themes the way Alice did. She liked a little mayhem.

"Another water slide?" he asked. The new one burst out of the fourth floor and snaked around the building only to disappear through an exterior wall on the ground floor.

"Helen said they got it a two years ago." She shook her head, smiling the same smile he imagined he had on his face. Like it was all just so damn good. Good to see. Good to *feel.* "I'd forgotten how big this place is."

He turned off the car, and in the silence the truck felt smaller. Snow landed on the windshield and melted, running down the glass.

"Why haven't you been back, Josie?"

She looked over at him and he saw how complicated it all was. The same complicated that had made him want to leave the other morning.

"It's not...all because of me and that night?"

"That's part of it," she answered. "But part of it is also my job."

"Because you're busy?"

"Yeah, and my mom just can't keep her opinions about it to herself. And defending my choices every time I see her is a drag. And..." She took a deep breath and let it out slowly. "I don't know. I guess...I'd put the Riverview away."

"Away?" he asked with a laugh, like he didn't know

exactly what she meant. Like it didn't strike some deep chord in him, too. No, he thought, he didn't want to fall backward into that place they'd occupied—knowing each other's thoughts before they were words. Knowing each other's experiences because they shared such a similar way of being in the world.

"I made them come to me," she whispered. "Visiting me in the city because I was so busy. They were busy, too, building this place…"

"But they visited you?"

She nodded. "I acted like my work was more important and, I mean, look at how wrong I was."

"Not everything has to be important," he said.

"That sounds ridiculous." She rolled her eyes at him.

He shrugged. "I don't know. I'm sure *I Do/I Don't* is important to its viewers. You know, who are looking for something mindless to take them away from whatever hard reality they've got happening."

She looked at him for a long moment and then smiled. "You always were good at that."

"At what?'

"Making me feel better."

The front door of the farmhouse was thrown open, and there was Helen looking nervous.

"She planned this, you know," he said, leaning forward so he could see her out of Josie's window. He felt Josie's breath on his cheek, the skin of his neck.

"Helen is always planning something," Josie said.

"You mad at her?"

"Are you?" Josie asked, turning to look at him, and their faces were inches apart. Not even.

"No," he whispered, his eyes on her mouth. Remembering so clearly what she'd tasted like that night. Artificial fruit salad. And now she would taste like Chapstick and coffee. Maybe the lasagna he'd made with his own hands. "I'm glad she brought me back. I missed this place."

And you. He didn't say it. Largely because it didn't need to be said. It just was. Like breathing. Like the beauty of Christmas at the Riverview Inn.

"We...we should go," she said, opening the truck door and letting in the freezing cold air. She was about to slip out but he grabbed her hand. Too much, maybe, but he had to know where things stood. It felt a little like he was pushing on something that he shouldn't be pushing on.

But at the touch of his hand on hers, she stopped.

"I wish I knew how to not hurt you," he said, and she looked up at him.

"You're not hurting me," she whispered.

"They why are you running...?"

"I'm not hurt," she said. "I'm scared."

"Of me?" He sat back, putting as much distance between them as he could. "I'm sorry. I swear—"

This time it was her hand reaching for his. The cold air made plumes of their breath. But when her fingers touched his they were warm.

"I'm scared of what you make me feel, Cameron," she said with a wry twist to her mouth. "I always have been. And that...I mean, I can't believe it, but it hasn't changed."

"What do I make you feel, Josie?"

She smiled, but it shook at the edges. She blew out a long breath and it, too, was shaky. "Everything," she answered. "You make me feel everything. Everything I told myself I didn't want to feel anymore."

13

———

MAX

The ceiling had nothing to say. It never did. He'd been staring up at this ceiling since Cameron left all those years ago and not once had there been any insight from it or the fan or the spiderweb in the corner.

It was just him and his mistakes.

"Max?" Delia's sleepy mumble at his shoulder made him turn his head.

"Go back to sleep," he whispered and kissed her forehead.

"What time is it?"

He looked toward the window, the sheers lighter now than then they'd been when he initially woke up.

"Seven, maybe?"

She groaned and burrowed closer to him, and he could feel her, the way he always did, fall back to sleep. The slight loosening of her body, the easing of her mind. All the energy that was Delia awake, but turned down several notches.

We made a mistake, he wanted to say. No, that wasn't right. *I made the mistake. All those years ago. I made a terrible mistake.*

He eased away from Delia, replacing his body heat, which was what Delia primarily wanted him for on these cold mornings, with the quilt, tucking it up around her shoulders.

She smiled in her sleep and he ached with love for her.

With the love he had for what they had built.

He'd spent the first year after Cameron left telling himself that he'd made the decision because he was protecting his family. All while missing Cameron with a pain so sharp it hurt to take a deep breath—like Cameron somehow wasn't part of his family. Wasn't the first son he'd always dreamed of, long before Dom came into being.

The house was quiet and cool and he walked into the kitchen expecting to find Josie beating her laptop into submission. But the kitchen and living room were empty. He walked back toward her bedroom but the door was open, the covers on her bed hastily pulled back up.

Dom was in his room. His gigantic son with the wicked slap shot and the subversive sense of humor. His feet hung off the bed and his head was buried in the pillows, only his hair visible.

What would I have done if it had been Dom in Cameron's position?

The answer, to his great chagrin, was—everything different. He would have protected him and talked to him about everything that happened. There would have been more conversation. Not less. More support. Not less.

He walked back into the dark kitchen.

Snow was starting. Christmas Eve was in two days and the forecast was calling for snow every one of those days.

Cameron, if he was going to leave, or Josie, if she was going to leave, weren't going to be going anywhere after today.

Was that good or bad? he wondered.

Years ago, after the shooting that had cost him his job in the city, after he'd made that horrible mistake and a whole family had had to pay for it, he'd lived in this kind of...blank space. He tried very hard not to think anything. Or feel anything.

Delia and Josie had pulled him out of that into a Technicolor, wildly and deeply emotional world.

And he'd been grateful for it every day. Like, on his knees grateful. But every time he looked at Josie, he saw the same kind of blank space. Yeah, she was busy and important and doing a job that she seemed to like...but that look in her eyes. He recognized it. And last night he'd seen it in Cameron.

I'm not your employee anymore.

God, the words had been bullets right through his heart. But the look in Cameron's eyes had been worse. All that distance Cameron and Josie were putting between themselves and the world. All that distance between themselves and love.

Max had some work to do. He was still the Family Officer for the county and Christmas was usually a time when kids got into trouble. No school to keep them occupied. Home lives in trouble. So he and Dante at the parole office had been trying to keep some of the most at-risk kids in the area busy. Delivering food. Shoveling sidewalks. The usual.

As he opened up his email, he remembered so clearly how he'd been desperate to do the same for Cameron. And how Cameron had fought and fought and fought...

Until he got tired. The way so many of those kids got

tired. Of pretending they didn't need love and boundaries and to use their bodies and brains and be respected for what they could do.

And then Alice had taken Cameron into the kitchen and it had been game over for the boy. He'd found himself, found something he cared about and someone to help him learn it.

And I took all of that away.

The guilt was a fresh hot spike in his chest.

Max and Dante exchanged emails regarding some shoveling they were planning to do in town in the next week and which kids they were going to get involved. He wondered if Cameron would be interested in helping out. After all those years of fighting Cameron was the first guy to sign up for these kinds of thing.

But then he wondered if Cameron would still be here in a week.

If he was still here now.

And suddenly he had an urgent need to know. To see the kid. To try, the way he hadn't been able to the previous night, to repair what had gone so wrong between them.

He closed the laptop, left the rest of the coffee for when Delia woke up, and shrugged into his coat. It had been a long time since he'd been down at the lodge in the morning, but he found himself looking forward to it.

Alice's bread, the black tar she pretended was coffee. The hum and business of the kitchens. Dad coming in to light the fires.

And Cameron.

Snow was falling, and so he skid a little when he braked at the stop sign. Turning on his right blinker, he saw the taillights to a van heading left down the road, toward Daphne and Jonah's place.

"Shit," he muttered, hoping he hadn't missed his chance.

The snow was coming down hard, and when he parked in the back, where the van usually sat, the snow was already filling in its tracks. The air smelled cold and crackly, which usually meant they were going to get a real storm. Josie had used Delia's truck to come down here at dawn, apparently, and he parked beside it.

In the time it took him to walk from the truck to the back door, snow had gathered in his hair. Along his jacket.

The warmth of the Riverview kitchen enveloped him the way it always did, like arms coming around him. The smell of coffee, lasagna, and bread didn't hurt.

"If you're looking for the kids you just missed them," Alice said, wiping off the last of her big baking trays and putting it in the rack beside the oven.

"I'm guessing you mean Cameron and Josie?"

She smiled, one side of her mouth lifting as much with bitterness as with joy. "Coffee?"

"Sure."

"Lasagna?"

"For breakfast?"

"Like you don't want it."

He pulled out one of the stools at the island and sat. Alice poured him a cup and brought him a slab of lasagna that practically hung over the edges of the plate. He picked up his fork but couldn't quite find the will to eat it.

"You all right?" she asked.

"No," he said. " You?"

"I spent the morning cooking with Cameron. I didn't think that would ever happen again."

"Yeah," he said. "I don't suppose you did." They sat in silence.

"You have something you want to get off your chest?" she asked him.

"Do you?" he shot back.

She poured herself the last of the coffee and sat down at the island beside him.

"We handled that night all wrong," he said. Alice nodded.

She swallowed, so clearly carrying such a load on her shoulders. He'd grown used to living with women after so many years of just him and his brother and dad, and he knew the therapeutic importance of hugs.

But Alice wasn't a hugger.

He covered her hand with his and she immediately grabbed him, holding on tight.

"They loved each other."

"I know."

"A real and honest love."

Shit. "I know."

"And even if it never became anything more, they deserved a chance to have that first real love. That first love is how you learn to love. And how you learn who you are in love. And how to live inside it. And we...we took that away from them."

"We broke up their friendship. And they needed each other," he said. "Josie...I feel like Josie has been so alone since he left."

"And it feels like Cameron has just put everything that happened before he left...away. We started a five questions interview yesterday and I brought up his mom and it was like..." She shook her head. "...I'd smacked him."

"I asked for his help last night and he said he wasn't my employee anymore."

"He may never forgive us."

"But what about Josie?"

"They left here together to deliver the food."

"They did?" In his chest he felt a flicker of hope. He had a lot of reasons to both trust and distrust hope. It was fickle and could turn on a person on a dime. But if he'd learned anything in these years with Delia, making a family, building a home, it was that if you didn't have hope—even when you feared its eventual extinction—you had nothing.

"They were smiling."

He blew out a breath. "That's something."

"Let's not start congratulating ourselves yet. We still have a mess to clean up."

JOSIE

There was always a lot of mayhem at Haven House. And even though the school and offices were officially on break, there were a lot of families there.

A lot of kids.

And it was like Christmas had barfed all over the place. Kids' drawings and paper chains and holiday lights covered every square inch of wall.

"I forgot about this part!" Josie said as she and Helen and Cameron carried food into the dining room while kids rushed by. She lifted a tray of lasagna up so it didn't bean a kid in the head.

"Hold up!" Daniella, an older Black woman who was once a resident and was now the day-to-day manager of the kitchen, stopped the kids at the end of the hallway. "You turn yourselves around and go help them bring in the food."

The kids turned, faces beaming, and started running back toward them. "Walk!" Daniella shouted, and the kids immediately slowed down.

"That is a superpower," Cameron murmured.

"Oh, it smells so good," Daniella said. "Bring it in. Bring it on in."

They stepped into the kitchen, which was a larger version of the one in the Riverview since the remodel a few years ago. It looked big enough to hold all the cooking classes it could run.

They set down the lasagna and the kids came running in after them with foil-wrapped loaves of bread in their arms.

Helen brought up the rear with the salad. "There's still more in the van."

Cameron and Josie walked out of the kitchen and into the hall, their shoulders bumping each other, and Josie shifted away, suddenly self-conscious, and stepped behind him.

"You okay?" he asked.

Just completely and totally in my own head and making a fool of myself. "Just fine!" she said over-brightly, deeply rattled by what had happened in the truck. He shot her a quizzical grin and opened the door to the snowy cold outside. They brought in the last of the food. And Helen and Daniella were strategizing in the kitchen, figuring out the timeline for dinner and delivery to the church.

"Are we going to deliver food in town?" Cameron asked.

"The roads are too bad," Daniella said. "We're gonna feed everyone here tonight and hopefully deliver tomorrow."

Cameron nodded, though he was undoubtedly imagining what Alice would have to say about the shape her salads would be in by the next day.

"But don't you worry," Daniella said with a bright twinkle in her eyes. She was the kind of short woman who always seemed taller on account of all her personality and power. "I've got a job for you."

"Wrapping," Cameron said. "I knew it."

"It won't be that bad," Josie said, reaching over to push on his arm.

"You know, you say that every time, and every time it is paper-cut city."

"Well, come on," Daniella said, leading them from the kitchen down another hall to the meeting room that always got taken over for presents and wrapping.

"You coming?" Josie asked Helen over her shoulder.

Helen shook her head, a smile teasing her lips. "I think you two have it covered."

Josie stepped back into the kitchen.

"Don't," she said in a low voice.

"Don't what?" Helen asked innocently.

"Don't be too pleased with yourself," Josie said. "This could have gone another way entirely." She thought of Max and Cameron, and the tension between them, and the tension she still had with Alice. "It still could."

Helen sobered. "You should have been friends all this time. I was just trying to make something that was really wrong a little bit right."

Yeah. Josie knew that. And, frankly, she was glad her friend had staged this reunion. Whatever happened next. Seeing him again was so sweet. "Thanks," she said, squeezing her friend's hand. "It is really good to see him."

"See him?" Helen asked, waggling her eyebrows.

"It's not like that," Josie said, not quite able to hide her blush.

"Oh, honey," Helen said. "Between you two, it's always like that."

Uncomfortable with that insight, Josie left the kitchen

and walked into the meeting room where Cameron was sitting on the floor surrounded by red and white wrapping paper and silver bows and long silver ribbon. Bows the size of Josie's hands. And on one side of the room were stacked presents. Presents for the kids and moms in Haven House and other presents for families in town that needed help getting something under a tree.

"That...that's a lot of gifts," she said.

"Paper-cut city," he said, shaking his head. "We better get to work."

THE SYSTEM WAS SIMPLE. Kids got green paper. Grownups got red paper. Silver ribbon for men. White ribbon for women. The kids' ribbons were differentiated by age, not gender. Lots of Legos. Lots of books. Lots of science kits and bubbles and new hats and warm mittens. Jumping ropes and art supplies.

"Didn't you come up with this ribbon system?" Cameron asked as they got down to business. They sat cross-legged beside each other, just like they always had. Knees touching. Reaching across each other for paper and tape.

"I did. Probably my single greatest achievement. Do you have the tape?"

He gaped at her. "You seriously just had it."

"I know, but—"

"It's under your knee."

She stuck her tongue out at him like they were kids, and they settled into a rhythm she hadn't felt in years.

"I was engaged," he said. And it was like a needle scratching over a record. She felt those words in the back of her brain. "And my fiancée's mother used to make these tiny, incredibly intricate dolls out of paper. She tried to

teach me once but got so frustrated she had to walk away.
"

He taped the paper down on a box of Legos and, without measuring, cut the paper to cover the rest of it. She gasped in horror.

"What?" he said.

"You've got to measure."

"What? It's fine..." He folded the paper over the rest of the box, but it didn't come close to matching up and most of the Lego logo was visible. "I'll just cover that up with another piece of paper."

"Or you could do this totally revolutionary thing and measure the paper around the box before you cut."

"Yes. I could do that."

"But you're not going to?"

He untaped the cut paper and measured it around a smaller box and started wrapping that. Josie shook her head, laughing at him.

Silence settled down around them and it didn't seem like he was going to bring up the fiancée. She told herself not to do it. What good could come of knowing the kind of woman he'd loved enough to want to marry? "Who was she?" Internally she winced. "Your fiancée?"

He blew out a breath. "A doctor in Kenya. We met about nine months after I left the States. And we had a few months of being pretty happy before we realized we'd made a mistake and we split up, amicably."

"Really?"

"No. She broke my heart but good." He smiled at Josie and she saw that he was joking, but it was true, too. And she forced her face to smile.

"I had been traveling for a year when we met and I was

ready to settle down. I wanted children and a house, and I thought she wanted the same."

"She didn't?"

"She'd gotten a four-year grant to study retinoblastoma in children living in remote villages in Burundi."

"You didn't want to go?"

"No, I would have gone. But it was painfully obvious she didn't want me to. She wanted to focus all her energy on her work and…" He shrugged. "I respected her for it. And bowed out."

"And you've never gotten close again?" she asked.

"No." He set the wrapped present in the stack of gifts with green ribbons. "What about you?"

"Me what?"

"Come on, now, Josie. I told you."

"No one. Really." She focused all of her attention on the pretty, warm slippers she was wrapping for some lucky mom.

"I'm not believing that. Smart and beautiful and kind and funny—you had guys mobbing you in high school."

"I was just so busy, I guess."

"Too busy to date?"

"I don't know, Cameron. I had a crush on you in high school, graduated and developed a complex that I'd sexually harassed you and gotten you kicked out of the only home you ever had, so I didn't really know how to be…casual. Or even available for any of that."

His silence was stunned and she didn't look at him for a long time. Her plan had backfired. Magnificently. But soon his silence became unbearable and she glanced up to see his open-mouthed astonishment.

"What?" she asked, not liking the way he was looking at her. "I should have been different? I should have handled

you leaving better? I was mourning you, Cameron. I was—"
Oh god, she was going to cry. She pressed her fingers to her
eyes and wished she had a tissue for her nose that was
suddenly dripping. Great. Just great.

"Hey," he whispered. And he was right there. She could
feel him there. The warmth of his body and his breath. His
heart.

"I'm fine." She took a deep breath and did what she did
best—smiled her way through it. As long as she didn't look
at him or...touch him, she'd be fine.

"Josie?" And then the jerk had to go and touch *her*, his
fingers against her chin. Pulling her face up so she had to
look into his eyes while bearing the incendiary heat of his
hand.

Stop, she wanted to say. *Stop making this so hard.*

But when her eyes met his she saw clearly what he saw.
What the family didn't see. Her friends and coworkers.

"Have you been alone all this time?" he asked.

14

———

JOSIE

She pushed his hand. "You know something? Screw you. Screw you and your doctor fiancée. And your judgment. You left. You left me. Without one word, Cameron." She smacked at his hand and got to her feet.

"What are you...Josie!"

She was at the door, her hand on the knob. No plan but to get away from him. Tears burning her eyes and words burning in her throat.

He grabbed her again, her hand in his, and she pulled away but he wouldn't let her go.

"Cameron," she snapped, not wanting to yell. Just wanting to leave.

She pushed him, but he didn't let go and she toppled forward as he stepped back and then...god, if she wrote it, it wouldn't be believed...she collided into his body.

"I'm sorry," he whispered. "I'm sorry. I am. I am so—"

Her hand curled into a fist and her plan, her instinct, was to smack him right across the face. The way he'd taught her when she was sixteen and was going on a date she didn't want to go on with Tom Pinkton. But at some point the electric impulse in her brain to slap him changed, shifted.

Ignited.

"You asshole," she breathed.

And she kissed him.

She kissed him like a smack. Like she wanted to do violence. And he received the kiss like he knew. Like he was going to absorb all her anger and turn it into pleasure. Give her back some of the things he'd taken away when he left.

Things he didn't even know about.

"Breathe, Josie," he whispered against her mouth, and she realized she was holding her breath. She gasped and then went back for more, wrapping her hands in the fabric of his T-shirt and pulling him toward her. Their lips met like they'd never been apart. And maybe he'd been dreaming of this kiss for as long as she had. Replaying those messy teenage fumbles until the memories were threadbare. His fingers clenched in her hair and he slipped his tongue into her mouth. She moaned, the anger leaving. Fading. Dissipating to mist in the heat between them.

This, her body sighed.

This, her brain marveled.

This, her heart warned.

This was what she'd been missing. What she'd kept hoping she would feel anytime another man kissed her. This full body shiver and delight. This deep from her belly *craving*.

She dated actors and athletes, men who routinely showed up on lists of New York's hottest bachelors. And they left her cold.

How ridiculous that the only man who'd ever made her feel this way was *him*.

Cameron.

There was a knock on the closed door of the room and she pushed him away hard. And so fast, he nearly fell over. Adrenaline made her shaky and she bent down to gather up the presents they'd wrapped so she wouldn't have to look at Helen as she came in.

"Hey," Helen said. "The snow is really coming down and Maria just came back from town and said the roads are really slick."

"Yeah?" Cameron said. "Josie, we should maybe—"

"Go. Before it gets worse," Helen said.

"Okay," Josie stood, projecting the unkissed, unruffled version of herself. "We're mostly done with the presents."

"Alice has canceled dinner tonight," Helen told them, looking down at her phone. "Did you get her text? Everyone is fending for themselves. Cinnamon rolls in the morning."

"I guess I know what I'll be doing tonight," Cameron said and then read the text from Alice.

Everyone is staying in homes tonight because of storm. Make cinnamon bun dough tonight? All the stuff in the usual places.

"It's like nothing has changed," Helen said, and Cameron, still smiling at his phone, nodded.

Josie and Cameron put on their coats, pulled on their hats, and made very, very sure they never actually looked at each other.

And then they were in the truck. The doors slammed. The silence an echo.

"Josie," he said.

"Just drive," she said.

CAMERON

The sky was dark, and the snow was thick and wet on

the ground. He pushed the truck into four-wheel drive, grateful the old lady still had it where it mattered. He took tiny glances at the stone-cold woman sitting next to him. Looking at her he couldn't believe that five minutes ago she'd been holding onto him hard enough to leave bruises.

Hard enough to make him think she wanted him as much as he wanted her.

"I can drop you at your parents'," he said.

"My laptop is at the lodge," she said.

He felt, suddenly, like a teenager, reading into what she was saying. Finding codes and messages in the tilt of her head. The clench of her hands in her lap.

The thing was, in his head, the closure of sex wasn't as easy now. Now that he imagined her, for the last five years, alone. Sex, which usually felt like the most balanced, natural thing in the world, now felt...loaded and unfamiliar.

The lodge was quiet when they got there. Alice wasn't in the kitchen. The fireplaces were cold. Through the back windows he could see Alice and Gabe's cottage nestled into the V of the rolling hills, partially hidden by trees. The windows were lit up against the gloom, smoke rose from its chimney.

Snow was coming down hard and fast, gathering in the corners of the windows.

"Hello?" he cried. No one answered.

They were alone. And he didn't know what to do. A grown-ass man completely thrown into chaos by this woman the girl he'd loved had turned into.

"Grab your laptop," he said. "And I'll take you home."

Behind him she was silent and he turned, not wanting to hope. But she stood there, her desire plain on her face. He realized that seven years ago she'd said everything, pulling her confessions and feelings up by the roots to present to him. And he'd stayed silent. Or made promises about a day that had never come.

It was his turn to tell her a few things. Things he never got to say.

"You're so beautiful," he told her, and the corner of her mouth lifted.

He crossed the room to stand in front of her. Close enough to touch if she wanted it. He watched as he got nearer how her breath came in tighter and smaller, how she fisted her hands and then relaxed them at her sides, only to do it again like she wasn't sure what she wanted to do with them.

"I loved—"

She kissed him. Threw herself at him, really, like the girl she'd been, and he caught her against him like a man who'd been handed a dream. A dream he had to hold onto at all costs.

Oh god. She was going to be the end of him. The absolute end.

"Take me upstairs," she said.

"Are you sure?" he asked. "Because we don't—"

Had that been him this morning? Thinking sex would be easy? Was he that fool?

"Please, Cameron," she whispered.

Yeah. Game over. No more talking.

He lifted her against his body, her feet dangling over the floor, and carried her toward the stairs. Her hips bumped against his, that sweet roll, and he was hard between one breath and the next.

At the stairs he set her down and they ran, hand in hand, up the stairs to her room. That last room on the right where family always stayed at the inn. The room where it had all happened.

She hesitated, her hand clenching round his fingers.

"It's just a room," he said. Because he knew exactly what she was feeling.

"You're right."

And then they were inside. The curtains drawn across the window gave the room a kind of murky glow. A muffled quiet.

"Hi," he said, smiling down at her face, so familiar.

"Hi." Her smile was sweet.

"Just so you know...I've been thinking about this moment for a solid chunk of my life and I have a list of things I need to do to you."

"Need?" she whispered.

"Yeah." He pulled her close, up tight against his body, and she let out a gasp. Surprised and turned on all at once. "For instance," he whispered. "I need to kiss you here."

He pressed his lips to the side of her neck, in that dip of tendons and bone where he could see her heart beating. "And here." The base of her throat, that sweet valley where her collarbones met. It had a name, that place, he just could never remember. "And here."

Her black shirt had buttons down the front and was made of some silky material, and he pressed a kiss to the place revealed by every V-neck T-shirt she wore in all the years he knew her.

"Cameron," she breathed, her head falling back. Her weight in his arms was complete.

"I'm just getting started," he said, and considering he was supporting her body in his arms and he had zero fucking patience left, he gathered one side of that silky shirt in his fist and just tore it open. The fabric ripped and the buttons bounced onto the hardwood floor.

The minor violence of it added gasoline to an already

hot fire. He kissed his way down to her breasts, taut and trembling in a no-nonsense bra. He pressed a hand to her stomach just to feel the muscles there quiver against his palm. He sucked her tongue just to feel the vibration of her moan.

She grabbed handfuls of his shirt, lifting it up until they had to stop kissing so she could pull it off, and the second's separation was too much and they fell back onto each other like they were starving. And all the tenderness he'd thought he'd feel when he imagined finally getting his hands on her was lost and it was just need between them. Need—and every year they'd spent away from each other.

"Yes," she moaned. "Hurry."

They got tangled up trying to take off each other's pants, and quickly gave up and worked on their own. Belts clanked and jeans were shoved out of the way and her hands, oh sweet god, her hands slipped over the gray fabric of his boxers. Her palm rubbed against the painfully hard length of his dick and he saw stars against the backs of his eyelids. He lost his own rhythm for a second and pressed his head against hers, standing there, letting her touch him the way he'd barely been able to dream of when they were young.

She slipped her fingers into the waist of his boxers, edging them down over the head of his cock and then off his hips. He sucked in air, suddenly light-headed.

"Watch," she breathed, and he opened his eyes and did as she asked.

Her hand curled around his shaft and it was everything. *Everything.* His breath sawed in his chest.

"I wanted this," she said. "Even before I really knew what it was."

Yes. Yes. He understood that. A snake brain longing when they were too young to really know.

"I wanted to kiss you and touch you, and I wanted to be kissed and touched by you," she said.

He kissed her forehead. She circled her thumb around his dick.

"You really are so beautiful." She stroked him, over and over, and he stood there and took it for as long as he could. Holding on to control by a thread until it suddenly snapped in her fingers, and it was stop her or come all over her belly.

He grabbed her hand, taking it off his body.

"Cam—"

"I know. But I've got some things I need to do."

Her laugh was a quiet humph. "Like what?"

He picked her up again by the waist, kissing her and walking her backward toward the bed, toppling them both onto it. Her legs parted and he slid into the cradle of her hips like this was a dance they'd done a million times.

Her legs wrapped around his waist and his cock rocked against her. He held his breath and pushed aside his own reactions, studying hers. Listening to how her breath broke and noticing when she shuddered and shook.

He cupped her breast and she sighed. He sucked her nipple and she cried out. He bit her nipple, just a little, and her entire body arched against him.

Yes. Yes. He was learning her. They way he'd always wanted to. And when his fingers slipped down over her stomach into her damp underwear he found her wet and hot. Her skin flushed and her eyes closed and he watched her face as his fingers found the spot that made her tremble against him.

"Yes," he breathed, feeling like he'd cracked a code or unlocked a safe. Here she was open and on the edge at the very tips of his fingers. He stopped and her eyes flew open.

"Just checking," he breathed.

"Please. Please, Cameron."

And now he was cracked open. Totally revealed. His name on her lips in just that way was the end of him. Abruptly he stood.

"What—?" she gasped, as if he'd yanked some rug out from under her.

"Condom."

She blinked, her mind gone in some anticipatory haze. Some half-finished blown-out bliss, and he smiled at her and felt himself slipping. His very protected idea of what exactly this was between them losing it edges.

Fuck her and move on. That had been the plan. Answer the question that had burned in the back of his brain for so long: What would we be like together? And walk back out the door. Maybe they'd stay in touch this time. He could visit her when he found himself in New York City.

Or not.

But looking at her on that bed, his fingers still damp, his mouth still tasting like hers, he thought the worst thing he could think right now. *She would be so easy to love. Again.*

"Cameron?" She pushed herself up to her elbow and then onto her hand. "Are you okay?"

So strange that the only person he could talk to about this was her. *I'm in trouble,* he wanted to say. *I'm in a lot of trouble with you.*

"Good," he said and went into the bathroom to get the condoms. His dick was so hard it hurt.

He came back to the bed and tossed the condoms down beside her on the bed. She grabbed one as he grabbed her hips, pulling her down to the edge of the bed.

"Wha—?"

"This."

His knees on the floor, he pulled off her underwear,

damp and thin. And then he settled himself between her thighs he could taste her before putting his mouth on her. And he knew she was about to become his favorite flavor. That, years from now, he'd wake up from a dream and still be able to taste her.

He put one arm over her hips, the tip of his tongue tracing her delicate seam. She jerked and moaned, and he did it again, deeper each time, until he was inside of her.

She pulled at his hair, pushed at his head.

"I'm going to—"

He hummed against her, slipped his finger deep pushing on that soft tender spot as he sucked her clit and she exploded against him, a shaking, wild dance between him and the bed. She clapped a hand over her mouth, her eyes closed, and she tried to control it as best she could which was cute. Sure.

But also not going to work for him.

If he was in danger of falling apart, he needed her right with him.

And there was no one in the goddamn lodge.

He grabbed a condom and slid it on, and before her orgasm had faded he pushed himself deep.

She hissed a pained breath. Her face twisted in a sharp wince.

"Am I hurting you?" he asked, pulling out, noticing just how tight she was.

"I'm fine," she lied.

"Bullshit, Josie. I'm…" There were faint smears of blood on the condom and his heart stopped. Dead.

"Please," she moaned, lifting her hips to tempt him back inside but he could not forget her blood. "Cameron. It just hurt for a second. I'm fine. I'm good. I need you. Please."

"How alone were you?" he asked, unable to believe he

was asking this. Unable to believe the answer he already knew in his gut.

A virgin. Josie had been a virgin.

She shook her head. Her chest was damp with sweat. Her eyes wide and dilated. "Don't stop. Please, Cameron."

"Goddammit, Josie." He bit the words out through his teeth. Everything inside of him was crumbling. Melting. He pushed back into her, slowly, so slowly. Taking care even when his control felt razor thin.

Her eyes popped wide and her hand left her mouth to grab onto the bedspread like she was about to fly up and away and needed the grounding.

"A virgin," he whispered, bending his head, clinging... clinging. "A goddamn virgin."

Savagely, he loved it. Loved it. That she was his in this way. It was backward and base, but it was real in him. A prehistoric delight.

He moved slow but all the way. As deep as he could go until he saw her eyes roll back in her head and the skin of her neck turn red. Her legs twitched restlessly against his and he grabbed her knees, pushing them back and onto the bed.

His plan had never been tenderness. His plan had been cathartic mutual violence.

Now it was survival.

He eased into her like this was the end. Like it was good-bye. Like it already hurt.

She grabbed his shoulders, breaking the distance he was trying to hold onto, and he lay against her, chest to chest.

"So good." Her breath hitched. "Oh my god, it's so good."

He ducked his head and got pulled into the rhythm of the orgasm that had been gathering in his body for— seven years? It was undeniable now, and he reached between them, found the bead of her clit, and worked it with his thumb. Harder than before. Finesse was gone and she jerked under him, her moans louder, but it wasn't enough.

He knew, all at once, that nothing would be enough. Not ever again. Not with her. Not without her. He was ruined. But that was a problem to deal with later. After.

"I want you screaming," he said.

"Cameron," she gasped.

"More."

He did as she asked, gave her more, holding on by a thread until her mouth opened on a sweet cry, her body a sweaty clamp of muscle and pleasure all around him, and he ducked his head, pushed his whole soul right into her, and came so hard he saw his life and his world explode into stars.

15

———

JOSIE

Whatever she'd thought the aftermath of sex with Cameron would be like, this...this wasn't it.

They lay, side by side, naked on top of the covers despite the chill in the air, catching their breath.

Carefully, so carefully, *not touching.*

How was that possible? How did he go from being inside of her to not touching her at all?

Is this me, she wondered, *not touching him? Or him not touching me?*

She grabbed his hand, a test, and he shifted out of the way. So far out of the way he got up and walked to the bathroom. Boneless and limp she watched him go, the flex and shift of his body was so beautiful her breath caught.

He's walking away. Again.

It's because I was a virgin. A twenty-four-year-old virgin. I knew that would be a whole thing.

And I should get up.

He came back into the room. He smiled at her. But it was...oh, it was off.

"You okay?" he asked.

"Yeah," she said and looked up at the ceiling, wondering why she felt like crying. "You?"

"Good. We....ah...should...talk about...what happened."

Oh god, he couldn't even say it.

"I should go," she said, because no. They weren't going to talk about it.

But the truth was, there was nowhere to go. He was silent and she felt her body go red and itchy, like she was having an allergic reaction to the moment.

Oh. After all this, it's like *that.*

Silence and more silence.

She got up off the bed and had to pause for a second to make sure her legs still held her, that her trembling, shaking muscles still worked. *How embarrassing*, she thought as Cameron calmly pulled on his underwear. Found his T-shirt and started to gather her clothes. She'd been fucked into some other state and he seemed...fine.

"Here," he said, handing her the shirt he'd ripped off her.

She shrugged it on but there was only one button left on it.

"Oh," he said, and she, nauseous with humiliation, slipped a hand over her chest. Covering the breasts still scraped red from his beard. *How*, she wondered, *was this happening?*

We weren't supposed to be like this.

She found her underwear and slipped it on, blinking back tears. There was blood on her thighs. Just a little. But there. She hid it by jamming her legs into her jeans. There'd be another shirt she could wear around here somewhere. A sweater left over a chair in the office or in the main closet. Lost and Found something.

Silently she opened the door. Her mouth clogged with tears and anger.

"Josie." He grabbed her hand and she jerked away. "This...this isn't going right."

"Well, that's...that's pretty par for the course with us, isn't it?"

"Look at me."

"Fuck you," she said without any heat.

"You are a virgin," he whispered, eyebrows raised, eyes pleading, like he was telling her she had cancer.

"Was," she said with a laugh.

He sucked in a breath. "This isn't funny," he said.

No. No, it wasn't.

"How was I supposed to let someone in after what happened?" *How was I supposed to let some other man touch me when I'd ruined everything?*

"I don't know." He was clearly baffled. "You just do. You move on."

"Like you did?" she asked and he was silent. "Well, I guess now I can. So, thank you for that."

She opened the door into the hallway, which was colder than the bedroom, and darker, too, somehow. The big windows at the end of the hallway looking out on the Catskills were shrouded in gloom.

She practically ran down the stairs.

"Josie." Cameron was following her.

"You don't have to do this, Cameron." She turned at the door, shoving her feet into her boots. She grabbed her jacket and her mitts from the hearth where she'd laid them out to dry. They'd both done that. Old habits walking into the Inn from a snow storm. You always set out your stuff or you'd be shoving your hands into wet mitts and no one liked that.

"You know, we answered the question we both have been asking for a long time."

"What would it have been like?" he said, standing there half naked and wholly attractive.

"Yep."

"And?"

"You were fine."

"Now who is talking bullshit?"

Me. I am. Total bullshit. I may never walk the same.

"Don't leave like this," he said.

She threw open the front door and let in harrowing blast of cold air so powerful she literally got pushed back a step. Snow gathered in a drift inside the door, and outside the door it was absolutely white. A blizzard.

Cameron jumped forward and shut the door, muffling the howling wind.

"Holy crap," she breathed and turned to look out the big windows. They showed nothing but a wall of white.

"It's a blizzard," he said. "Total whiteout."

His skin was gooseflesh and he blew air into hands that had to be freezing.

"I can't leave," she said.

They were snowed in.

CAMERON

He went upstairs to get dressed and check his phone and maybe...gather himself for a second. Man, the reality about a moment's hesitation was no joke. He'd screwed everything up. He rubbed at his eyes and slipped on warm socks.

Whiteout blizzard, Alice texted. *Tell me you're back at the lodge.*

I'm back, he texted. *Josie is here, too. We're fine.*

Okay. Storm's supposed to get worse until tomorrow morning. Stay in. I'll check in later.

He sent her a thumbs-up and went downstairs to assess the damage he'd done with that moment of silence.

And the plan. That stupid plan. Have sex with her and forget her. What was wrong with him?

Josie was sitting on couch in front of the empty fireplace, a blanket over her shoulders and her laptop open on her lap. She didn't even look up when he came in.

"Airports are closed," she said. "There's a twenty-car accident on the highway."

"Wow," he said. Because he was the king of conversation. The prince of cool. "Have you talked to your family?"

"Max was ready to put on the snowshoes and come look for us."

"You stopped him."

"Barely."

The moment seemed warm, a thaw between them, and he laughed. She did not.

"Josie—"

"I don't know how to talk to you Cameron. About this. About...us. So how about we don't?"

"Don't talk?"

"You did it to me before," she said, looking him straight in the eye, stone cold, and for a second he was impressed. How cool she was. How she worked so hard at indifferent. But he'd just tasted her body. Felt her breath break as she came. He knew this was pretend. The fury of her was all right there, shrouded in ice. "I have work to do," she said.

"No," he said.

She laughed. "No?"

"The truth is...I freaked out for a second. I wasn't expecting you to be a virgin and it...it threw me."

She rolled her eyes at him.

"It's the same way you're freaking out right now," he said. She looked back down at her laptop and he saw what she was going to do. How she was going to freeze him out.

He'd messed up. Sure. But they weren't going to go out this way. Not again.

He crossed the room and leaned down, bracing one arm on the couch beside her head, getting so far into her space that she had no choice but to look at him.

"I can still taste you in my mouth," he whispered and watched her eyes dilate, her lips part on a breath. "I can feel you against my body." He flexed his fingers. "On my skin. And I know you feel the same way. Because I know you..." She swallowed audibly and blood pounded to his dick. "You need a second. Okay. I can give you a second. Because I needed one, too. But we're not done. We will talk about this. We're not going to do what we did last time." He stood up, watching her face. Watching her heart pound in that part of her neck he'd coveted for so long. Now he knew how she tasted there. How that heartbeat felt under his lips. Against his tongue. "We have so much to talk about."

We're not done. We are far from done.

"You hungry?" he asked.

She blinked but was stubbornly silent. *Oh, the Josie silent treatment. I remember it well. Childish but effective.*

"You work, I'll be back." He turned toward the kitchen. There were the cinnamon rolls to start, and he thought about Josie and what he knew she'd eat.

But he also knew what she would love. He smiled. For almost every person the path to their heart was through their stomach. And for Josie, that path was made with cheese.

"Hey...Cameron?" He turned to see her. So small on the

big couch, swaddled in the blankets. Her pale skin surrounded by the fall of her dark auburn hair.

"Yeah?" What do you need? he wanted to ask. What do you want? Because he would do it for her. Anything. For her.

"Can you..." She looked at the huge stone fireplace, cold, the fire long since out. "Do you know how to build a fire?"

"I do," he said with a smile, and he walked back over to the hearth. "And I learned the same time you did." Max had taught them.

"I haven't made a fire in years," she said.

He sat on the stones, stirred the ashes to see if there were any embers. And there were. Hot and pink. He gathered kindling from the basket, built his teepee and blew gently, coaxing the embers to glow brighter. Hotter. The kindling caught and he slowly, patiently, fed it larger pieces of wood until it was kicking out proper heat and crackling away.

"There," he said, standing back.

"Thank you."

She was flushed and unable to look at him, and he walked out of the room wondering what kind of fire they were building. The kind that blazed hot and then turned to ash? Or one that would last?

And which one did he want?

Alice's kitchen was bigger these days, but not much else had changed. Everything was in the same general spot. Properly labeled. He pulled the stand mixer out and began making two doughs. The first, once prepared, he set to rise in a bowl covered with the old tea towel that had always been used for such things. Then he started on the cinnamon rolls. When that was done he blanched little purple potatoes he found in the cupboard. As well as some asparagus. He started mixing up goat cheese, feta, and shredded cheddar with a little bit of water.

When the first dough had doubled in size he punched it down, rolled it out, and created an odd-shaped boat, filled it with the cheese, brushed it all with melted butter, and put it in the oven to bake. He sliced up apples and found some cornichon pickles, carrots, and a couple of red peppers for dipping.

He made this food for her and tried hard not to think about all the years he'd dreamed of cooking for her. How long it had taken him to stop thinking *Josie would love this* after he tasted something new that blew his mind. Years. It had taken years for the ghost of her to stop traveling with him.

And now, after today, how long this time? he wondered. Before he stopped thinking about how she felt in his arms. Before he stopped thinking—*oh, I've got to tell Josie...* More years? Forever?

Could he survive that again?

Did he want to?

He took out the bread boat filled with melty cheese, slipped a raw egg yolk on top with a hunk of ice-cold butter. Loaded the dippers onto the tray with the bread boat and took it all into the living room.

"Something smells amazing," Josie said, looking up with a careful smile. He laid a tea towel on the ottoman, set the cookie tray on it, still hot but loaded with vegetables and potatoes and fruit, and then whipped the egg and butter into the cheese until it was all stretchy and perfect.

"What in the world is this?" she asked with the kind of wonder that made him happy.

"It's based on a Georgian dish that I had a million years ago. I've bastardized it here with the cheese Alice had, but the idea is all the same."

"A melted cheese bread boat?"

"Basically. The bread bakes while the cheese melts."

She dipped a slice of apple into the cheese, put it in her mouth, and closed her eyes with a moan. He smiled and looked away, fiddling with a pickle. "I'm sorry," he said. "About earlier. The truth is, Josie, I've spent—" he shook his head "—years thinking of what I would say to you after making love. Years. And in the moment...I freaked out."

He laid down his silence against her and waited for her to lay down hers. *Talk to me*, he thought.

"I get it," she finally said. "It's not like we planned this."

"Well..." He decided on painful truth. Absolute truth. They owed each other that. "The truth is, I might have been."

"Since when?"

"Really, probably the second I saw you when I first came in."

"You were going to have sex with me and...what...?"

"Say goodbye."

She set down the carrot.

"It was a bad plan," he said. More truth. Truth upon truth. "And maybe I created that bad plan because I don't know how to frame us. In my head. I don't know how to do... this." He waved a hand between them.

"Well, you did pretty great earlier." Her smile wobbled. "The sex part, anyway."

She was trying to make a joke, and he appreciated it but he couldn't laugh.

"We never got to tell each other how we felt," he said. "And I loved you, Josie. I really, really loved you."

Her breath hitched and broke and she sighed. "I loved you, too."

"So," he said, "my plan was stupid."

"Not stupid," she said. "The sex part was good."

"It really was," he said with a laugh.

"Really?"

There was something unsure in her voice and he looked at her with his eyebrows raised. "Josie," he murmured. "You can't have doubts about how good that was."

"Well, as you know, it's not like I have a lot of experience."

"Please tell me I didn't hurt you," he whispered.

"You didn't," she said. "It was just...a lot. All at once."

"How...?" He let it trail off because he didn't know how to ask the question.

"How am I a twenty-four-year-old virgin? Because it took me a long time to get over what happened the night of my birthday. And then, when other men touched me, I was just...so aware they weren't you. And then, I don't know, it got easier to simply turn it all off."

"Why now?" he asked.

"Because..." She sighed. "Maybe this is how we end. This is how we fix what went so wrong. And maybe it's how we become friends again. How we're in each other's lives again."

He held his breath, wondering what she was saying.

Does she want...?

"Not like a relationship. I mean, that wouldn't work. Even a little."

She laughed, and he smiled, though it stung. *Why not?* he wanted to ask. *What's stopping us from trying?* Her job? His lifestyle? Those weren't big problems. But her laughter indicated something else, something fundamental, and so he let the idea go.

"But as a goodbye?" She looked at him. "The goodbye we should have had? I don't know what would have happened that summer if we'd gotten together, but we were just starting our lives. And a goodbye between us was inevitable. And we never got to have it."

I would have followed you, he thought but didn't say. *I should have followed you*. Those were the things he never said out loud.

"This is goodbye, then?" he asked.

"I figure we have until our family comes barrelling through those doors."

"When the storm passes."

"Weather channel says we've got another day before the blizzard is over."

"A day? A whole day?"

It sounded good. Like a dream come true, really. And also like heartbreak all over again.

"How do you want to say goodbye?" he asked.

"Not by eating cheese," she said and kissed him.

16

CAMERON

Hours later, the room completely dark except for the fire crackling in the hearth, he brought the reheated cheese back to her where she lay on the couch, covered only by the blanket he'd tucked around her. She was at the edges of a puddle of warmth and light that they'd created. And—he wasn't going to lie—that he wished would never end.

He paused in the cold darkness, looking at her. How much time did they have left? An hour. Four? Six? Was that enough.

"Come on," she said, lifting the blanket. "You must be freezing."

"You are the prettiest thing I've ever seen," he said.

"That can't be true," she said, and he set down the food he'd made, pushed the ottoman closer so they could reach it, then scurried under the blanket with her. Her body was hot to the touch. She shrieked and flinched away from his cold hands but he wrapped his arms around her and pulled her close.

"Mean! So mean!" she cried.

"The cost of the Georgian cheese boat."

"Well, in that case…" She reached over and tore a piece off the bread boat and dipped it in the cheese. She handed it to him over her shoulder. As she reached for another one he could hear the buzzing and humming of her laptop where she'd slipped it beneath the couch.

"Were you working?" he asked.

"Just checking emails and…" He pressed the cold of his foot against her leg. "Yes. Yes. I was working."

He shifted his leg away but pulled her closer, the swells of her naked body filling the dips in his perfectly.

"I'm going to ask you five questions—"

"No!" She laughed. "Cameron, have you ever actually gotten to the fifth question?"

"With you? No. I don't think so. But hope springs eternal. Now, do you remember the rules?"

"Of course, Cam. I do watch your channel."

"As a reminder, you have to answer honestly and right off the top of your head. If you take longer than five seconds to answer you have to pay a penalty."

"That's new. What kind of penalty?"

"The kind I decide."

"You do love this game."

"Hey, it's served me well. Ready? What's the best part of your job?"

"Solving problems," she answered honestly.

"What's the worst part?"

She was silent.

"One…" He rolled her onto her back so he could see her face clearly. "Two." He lifted his hand, fingers extended and wiggling.

"Tickling?" she said. "Really? Tickling is the penalty?"

"Three."

He dug his fingers into her side, into that spot where she'd always been ticklish. And she did not disappoint. Howling and twisting, she tried to get away. "Okay. Okay!" she screamed, and he paused and repeated the question. "Worst thing about your job?"

"The people."

That made him pause. "You work with?"

"They're not bad. I mean, some of them are okay. But these contestants. Fame hungry and drama hungry, they make bad choices and we make bad choices and it just turns into...something ugly."

"Okay," he asked quietly. "Why do you do it?"

"Because they keep giving me more money and bigger credits."

"You never cared about money before."

She blinked at him. "Well, I grew up."

"You wanted to be a part of telling people's stories. That's what I remember. You were excited about working in film and television because you wanted that to be the medium for people's stories."

"That's not a question."

"Okay. What would you do if you could do anything?"

"Honestly, Cameron. I haven't thought about it."

"Why?"

"Because it would make me sad."

"Oh, Josie," he whispered, his heart breaking for her. "You gotta quit that job."

"And do what?"

"Figure it out."

"Are you telling me you're doing exactly what you want to do?"

He shifted, rolling over her, finding his way between her

legs where she was warm and welcoming. "Now I am," he said and kissed her. He kissed her and forgot that he had one more question to ask her.

JOSIE

Her body was toasty warm but her nose was cold. Without opening her eyes she tried to lift her hand to put it over her nose to warm it up, but her arms were caught against her body.

Cameron. Cameron was behind her on the couch, his arm over hers. His body heat under the blanket was like a furnace. Memories of the night curled through her. His lips. His hands. His body. The look in his eyes when she touched him. The way he said her name when she slipped him into her mouth. The grip of his hands on her hips. The growl of his voice when he told her how good she felt. How beautiful she was.

The remembered pleasure was this beautiful echo in her body, reaching out for her soul. Her heart.

This is goodbye, she told herself, because it didn't really feel like it. It felt like a second chance and she needed to remind herself it wasn't.

She blinked open her eyes and saw the fire was nothing but embers and bright sunlight was coming in through the big windows.

The sun was out. And long, long icicles were dripping from the roof down to the snow-covered ground. The mountains were blanketed in white.

She heard a very discreet cough, and her eyes flew to the edge of the fireplace closest to the door.

Patrick.

Patrick, who walked to the lodge early to light the fires

every morning in the winter. He stood there in his thick deerstalker cap and his red and black checked winter jacket. He was pink-cheeked from the snow. Or from finding his granddaughter naked on the couch with a man who had once been like a grandson to him.

Oh god, please just let me die.

"The storm stopped around seven a.m.," he said. "It's nearly nine now. Unless you want everyone to know your business, you might think about getting up." Then he started to blush. The tips of his ears got red. "I'll give you some privacy." He walked toward the kitchen and she immediately elbowed Cameron in the chest.

"Ouch," he said, keeping his eyes shut and trying to pull her back into his arms. "What's wrong?"

"It's nearly nine and the storm stopped two hours ago."

His eyes popped open. "Shit. Is anyone here yet?"

"Patrick," she all but wailed.

"Okay. Okay," he said. They threw off the blanket and in the chilly air of the lodge they scrambled into their clothes. She covered her torn shirt with an old flannel shirt of Max's that she found in the closet.

"I've gotta go to the bathroom," she said. "Can you...?" She waved a finger over the empty wine bottle and the glasses and the remains of the demolished cheese boat. Condoms. There were condoms in that mess, too.

"I got it," he said, and she ran for the stairs. As she hit the second floor landing she thought she heard him say her name, but when she turned he was already gathering up the mess and walking away from her.

CAMERON

He took a deep breath before walking into the kitchen.

Cameron was a full-grown adult and so was Josie, but that didn't make getting caught naked by a man he'd always considered a grandfather any easier.

He pushed open the door and found the old man standing at the coffee machine, watching as it gurgled and hissed.

"Hi Patrick," Cameron said.

"Hello Cameron." Patrick turned with a sparkle in his eye and Cameron found himself smiling.

"Probably not what you were expecting?" Cameron asked.

"Cam, I've been making the fire in this lodge every morning for years now and I've lost track of the number of times I've caught some family member naked."

"So nothing special then?"

"Well, I didn't say that." Patrick handed Cameron a mug.

Cameron set down the remnants of last night and took the coffee.

"I'm not supposed to have the high-octane stuff," Patrick said. "But I figure if no one is here to see me, maybe it doesn't count."

"I don't think it works that way."

"Probably not." Patrick took a sip of the brew made from Alice's very good beans and smacked his lips with delight. "So?" he asked.

"So?" Cameron echoed, looking for the milk because Patrick made his coffee like tar.

"So that's how you're going to play this?" Patrick asked. "Like it's no big deal?"

"There's no other way to play it," Cameron said.

"Says who?"

A thousand things rushed to his lips, but it was the truth that slipped out. "Josie."

Patrick's eyes went wide. "You made your move then?" he asked. "Stated your case."

"It's not that easy."

Patrick nodded sagely and took another sip of coffee before he set it down. "Well, I can't tell you your business," he said. "I wouldn't even pretend to know. But I will tell you what wasn't easy...for me." He pressed a gnarled hand to his chest, the wedding ring gleaming brightly against his wrinkled skin and oversized knuckles. A workingman's hand with a ring he'd never taken off.

"Yeah?" Cameron asked.

"All those years me and Iris spent apart. Because I'd convinced myself it was too hard to figure out how to get back together. How to forgive her. And help the boys forgive. How to forgive myself. It was all too hard. And I'd give everything I have for just one of those days back that we wasted. Because what's hard is loving someone when they're not here to be loved."

"Patrick," Cameron said. "We were kids when I loved her. It's not the same."

"Yeah. You were kids. But even then we knew what you two were. What you meant to each other. And maybe you are just friends. But I gotta tell you, son..." When Patrick called him son it didn't rankle like it did with Max. "I have not once gotten naked with one of my friends like you did with Josie." He waggled his old man eyebrows. "I've got to go make a fire. If someone comes, you made that coffee."

Cameron smiled and watched as Patrick left. *It's not the same*, he told himself when he found he wanted to believe it was. That Patrick was right—it was harder to be apart than to figure out how to be together. And maybe it wasn't hard for him. He had no ties to any place. No apartment. No job expecting him to solve problems twenty-four hours a day.

Stop. You knew the rules going in. This was goodbye.

He pulled out the cinnamon rolls that had proofed overnight and started to preheat the oven, and he did the dishes, and none of it mattered because he couldn't stop the thought that grew in his head.

What if this isn't goodbye?

17

———————

J OSIE
    She gave herself a minute in the bathroom. She brushed her hair. Found some mouthwash and made use of it. Washed her face and then pressed her face to a towel hanging on the back of the door and wondered what happened next.

What do I want to have happen next?

You gotta quit that job.

Not if she could change it, right? Not if there was a chance.

Fumbling, she pulled the phone that would not stop binging from her pocket. There were seven hundred new emails. Seven hundred. And nearly as many texts.

She scanned through the emails until she saw one from Network Executives, *Your Pitch* in the subject line. Her heart slammed up into her throat. It could work, all of this could work. She imagined opening the email, finding out they liked the idea and were looking forward to discussing it further after the holiday break. A fresh start. A new chance.

Her thumb opened the email.

We have no idea how this would even work, the email said. *Or what kind of audience might be into this? We would lose all of our advertisers. This might work in some kind of small setting but for our network it's a hard pass. You're very good at your job, Josie. And we look forward to you bringing this kind of energy to the new season of* I Do/I Don't. *Have a good holiday.*

There was a terrible blank spot where her heartbeat usually pounded. Where her brain made plans and lists and considered possibilities and opportunities. And then the blank space was filled with the hot burning rush of...not embarrassment. Not resignation. Anger.

Anger.

And not even at her bosses because, honestly, what had she expected?

What kind of fool was I to think they'd go for this idea? For any idea that wasn't a full asshole season.

You've got to quit that job.

That was incredibly obvious at this point. It was ludicrous, really, how obvious it was. Like all those things that had been so important to her were...well, meaningless. What she'd been clinging to, that hope, it was gone. And all that mattered was how painfully unhappy she was.

And she'd had just one day of happiness, bright and hot and beautiful, and now the idea of going back to that awful dark-gray place she'd lived in for the last few years was...*oh god.*

Looking at that email she knew there was only one thing to do.

They could give her money and make her queen of the world and it wouldn't change the fact that she was rotting from the inside.

She took a deep breath and sent an email to her boss.

This is my resignation. I'll help cast this season and then I'm out. Good luck.

Immediately she laughed. Immediately she was seven hundred emails lighter. The blinders were gone and she saw in the corners of her life a hundred possibilities and opportunities.

But there was only one right in front of her. Only one she really wanted.

She received an immediate response from her boss. More money. A better office. And none of it mattered.

She actually made some strange whooping noise in her throat. The relief of this...for a second she couldn't feel her hands.

She turned her phone off and put it back in her pocket.

The job she wanted was out in the living room. Or in the kitchen making cinnamon buns.

In the great room the fire was crackling but there was no sign of Patrick, who had undoubtedly made a quick escape. He liked a drama-free life these days. And Josie felt like she and Cameron had enough drama for a thousand people.

Suddenly there was Christmas music coming through the speakers and the lights on the tree were on. *Oh no*, she thought. *Not Alice. Not yet.*

But it was Cameron at the stereo. "It's the morning of Christmas Eve," he said. "The family is going to be here, like, any minute."

"Can I ask you five questions about your job?"

He blinked at her. "Sure."

"Where are you going next?"

"I haven't decided," he said. "I usually spend the winter in the Southern Hemisphere. Australia, maybe? But I need to finish the show with Mateo before I leave. And then I was trying to think of how to frame the Alice show. Maybe you can help me with that...you know...before you go back to the city."

I'd love to.

"Why do you take those meetings with Netflix and YouTube if you aren't interested in doing a show for them?"

"Because I hope when I'm in New York City I might run into you."

She smiled at him, shook her head. "There are easier ways to make that happen."

"I know that now. But it didn't seem so at the time."

"What are you hoping for when you take those meetings?"

"That they will pitch me an idea that sounds like me. That excites me."

"What if you went to them with a show idea? Created exactly the way you wanted."

"But they attach producers and writers, and then it gets co-opted."

"You happen to know a producer and a writer."

His mouth fell open for a second. "You want to work with me?"

The way he said *work* made it clear he didn't understand what she was saying. Or offering. And maybe that had been their problem all along. They never said what they meant. At least, not while sober.

"I just...quit my job. They're not interested in *Common Ground* and I can *not* go back to that place. You were right. I needed to quit. Not that that has anything to do with you. Or that you need to feel responsible. I should have done it ages ago. You just...pushed me in the right way."

"That's good," he said, very carefully.

"And I believe in you. In what you do. And I want to help. If that's...you know..." She was running out of steam.

"Something you want. I mean, I could take the next few months—I have savings—and help you create the show that you would want to do. That excites you. And then I can help you pitch it. If...you want...me?"

"Do I want you?" It was so bald. So plain. It made her scared. It made her doubt. Was she worth having? Was this ridiculous?

"Like that. Like...in your life in that way. In any way. You probably need to think about it. And I get that. I mean, it's Christmas Eve and we really...I mean, it's only been three days." She laughed, awkward and awful. "Anyway. It's just... something to think about."

"Josie." He took a step toward her. "I want to be clear. Is this a business proposition, or...more?"

"Both?" she whispered with a shrug, feeling as out of body as she'd ever felt. As she'd ever been. This was riskier than a kiss after her high school graduation. She'd never been so exposed.

He opened his mouth, but whatever he was going to say or do was crushed under the weight of the entire family storming into the lodge, loaded with presents and noise and distraction.

"You're alive!" Mom cried, bringing in the cold with her. "Take these, would you?" She unloaded a pile of brightly wrapped presents into Josie's arms. "Put them under the tree. I need to help Dom with the stockings."

Josie caught Cameron's eye before he was pulled into the kitchen by Alice, and the look on his face told her it was all too much. All too soon.

She'd driven him away. Again.

How is this a mistake I just keep making?

"Come on," Dom said, walking past her with rope in his hands. "Help me with the stockings."

Helen walked by, her brow furrowed, looking down at her phone.

"Are you all right?" Josie asked Helen.

"Fine. I just...haven't heard anything from Evan."

"Well, the storm."

"Totally, the storm." Helen put the phone in her pocket and took Josie in from the top of her head to her feet. "What have you been up to?"

"So much," she whispered.

"Yeah?" Helen asked, her eyes bright. She grabbed Josie's hand.

"But I just did something so stupid and I've ruined everything. Again."

"Josie!" Dom yelled from the fireplace. "You're helping me!"

"I gotta help."

"Yeah, yeah."

The stockings had once hung side by side on the mantel, but now there were too many so Max drilled little eye hooks into the wall, and the rope they hung the stockings on stretched from one corner of the room to the other. Ten feet of stockings.

"You okay?" Dom asked.

"Fine. Why?"

"You seem weird."

"You're a real wordsmith, Dom," she said.

"I don't know. Happy. I guess. You seem happy."

It was weird that it was true. Even if she had ruined everything with Cameron. Even if they weren't supposed to have more than one night, quitting her job had been the right thing to do. And she was happy. Even with heartbreak looming, she was happier than she'd been in ages. Years.

"I'm just so happy to be here," she said, surprised as the words came out of her mouth about just how true it was.

"You should come back more often," he said. "I mean. Mom and Dad, like...miss you."

"What about you?" she asked, advancing on her brother for a hug she knew he was going to try to wrestle out of. "Do you, like...miss me?"

"Yeah," he said. "I do." And then he surprised her by pulling her in for a hug.

"Oh, well, I miss you too, Dom," she said, squeezing him tight.

"Can we hang our stockings yet, or what?" little Iris asked.

"Hold your horses, Iris," Dom muttered.

She and Dom called all the kids to hang their stockings first. And then the grown-ups. A wall of stockings made of felt with names spelled out in sequins or ribbons. They were too small for all the things that got stuffed in them, and tomorrow morning there would be stacks of gifts beneath every one. Cookbooks and makeup, glittery nail polish and NHL bobbleheads. Warm socks and practical jokes. So much love made real, and Josie could not believe she'd wasted the last five years alone in her apartment when she could have been here. Here with all this tradition. And fun.

And love.

"You want to go tell Alice and Cameron it's their turn?" Dom asked.

"Yeah." And she knew it was time. Whatever was next with her and Cameron, it was time for Josie and Alice to be family again.

The kitchen was warm and delicious smelling, and Alice and Cameron were in there, moving around each other like they'd been doing it forever. Taking things in and out of the oven. Stirring pots on the stove.

"Taste this?" Cameron asked Alice and held out a spoon, his hand beneath it catching some kind of sauce.

"Perfect," Alice said after she sipped at the spoon.

"Well, that's a Christmas miracle," Cameron said dryly. "I don't think you've ever said something I've made was perfect."

"Well, I should have," Alice said.

"Another Christmas miracle!"

"It's your turn to hang stockings," Josie said abruptly from the doorway, her heart pounding a mile a minute. They both turned to stare at her.

"Do I still have a stocking?" Cameron asked, looking for all the world like the boy he'd been, surprised to be brought in out of the cold.

"Of course," Alice said, and the two of them started to take off their aprons.

"Actually," Josie said. "Can I talk to you for a second, Alice?"

There was a loaded moment in the kitchen, everyone looking at each other. They were the kind of moments she and her team used to spend hours trying to manage and create on the show. Pregnant pauses and dramatic silences. Josie stood there inside of it and held her own. Something she hadn't done for a really long time.

"Sure," Alice said and stayed back in the kitchen. Cameron walked by her, an eyebrow raised, and she smiled at him. Projecting things she wasn't sure she really felt. Calm. Control.

Cameron was gone; the sound of the family hummed on the other side of that door.

Alice rested a hip against the table. "Are you—?"

"In love with Cameron?"

"I was going to say *all right*." Alice blinked her eyes. "But we can go your way, too."

"I don't know. I don't know if I love him or if I never stopped loving him or if what I'm feeling is wrapped up in what happened. I don't have an answer for any of it."

"Okay."

"But I want to find out."

"That's good. Isn't it?"

"Are you going to stand in the way of it?"

Ah. Alice blanched white, her hand flittering from her hips to her face. "Is that...do you think that's what I want?" Alice asked.

"I've never been very good at understanding what you want. Or what you think. Or how you feel about me. But it's always been obvious you love Cameron. So, I'm asking you—"

Alice came striding across the kitchen to grab Josie by the shoulders. "You have my full blessing. My one hundred percent excitement and enthusiasm for you and Cameron being whatever it is you can be to each other. That's it. That's all. I love you both and just want to see you happy."

"Oh." Well, that took some of the wind out of her sails. Josie slumped in Alice's arms. "Well."

"I take it you two made the most of the snowstorm?"

Josie felt herself blush. And the need to tell someone, anyone, what she had done pushed the words right out of her mouth. And maybe Alice was the right person to bring this to. She knew Cameron better than anyone. Loved him unconditionally. "I think I just made this grand gesture and he's not interested in it."

"What was the gesture?"

"I quit my job and offered to help him create a show out of his YouTube channel."

"That is—"

"Ridiculous?"

"Perfect. Like the most perfect thing I've ever heard. Are you...all right?"

"I think so? I actually have no idea. I quit my job."

Josie laughed with hysteria and joy. Relief. Worry. All of it. She laughed and it caught on a sob.

"Don't tell my mom," Josie said. "I mean, I'll tell her, but she'll get all...mom about it."

"Come on. Sit. I'll put Baileys in your coffee and you can tell me all about it," Alice said. "And I promise to keep my mouth shut."

A week ago Josie would have said there was no chance for a relationship between herself and Alice, but she would have said the same thing about Cameron. And here she was, a welcome guest in Alice's kitchen. Spilling secrets and talking about the man they both loved.

Christmas at the Riverview Inn was full of strange possibility.

CHAPTER 18

CAMERON

The previous Christmas, Cameron had spent the holiday in Montreal with the skater. They'd walked through the Atwater Market and she'd broken her diet with smoked meat poutine and they'd had sex in the light from the Christmas tree. If you'd asked Cameron, he would have said it was about as good a Christmas as it got.

But standing in the mayhem of the Riverview Inn on Christmas Eve he knew he'd been lying to himself. This was what Christmas Eve should look like. And it should sound like twenty Mitchell relatives arguing over memories and playlists and which movies they were going to watch next.

It was his stocking, the one Delia had made for him ages ago, hung up on the rope next to everyone else's.

And it was his body, exhausted and relaxed from loving Josie all night long.

And his heart...oh god, this was how his heart was supposed to feel. Full. So full.

He turned away from the stockings and found Max at the door, prepared to go outside to get more firewood.

"Max?" he said, his mouth running twenty feet in front of him. "You going to get more wood?" He walked over to put on his boots.

"Yeah," Max said, not hiding his surprise and happiness.

"I'll help."

Outside it was the kind of cold that hurt to breathe. The icicles weren't dripping anymore—they'd frozen over again in the cold snap after the storm.

They walked around the side of the lodge to the old shed Max had been building when Delia and Josie first moved here. It was where they kept all the wood for all the fireplaces.

"Keeping this place stocked with firewood is still a full-time job," Cameron joked.

"You want it?" Max asked.

"No. I've done my time." Cameron was keeping it light, but the words held a certain weight. A hard reality. Max stopped and Cameron cursed himself. His mouth, again.

"I'd like to say something," Max said. "Without you arguing with me. Can I do that?"

"You can give it a try."

"I am sorry for my part in what happened seven years ago. If I'd acted any other way, we wouldn't have gotten to where we got so fast. We might have been able to talk—"

"I don't know, Max. You found me on top of your drunk, half-naked daughter. I'd have kicked me out, too."

Max looked down, his jaw working. And suddenly... suddenly, the moment wasn't hard. All the hard work of letting go of the past had been done sometime in the night. Or maybe this morning when Josie made the miraculous effort to create a way into the future for them.

"Max," Cameron said and stepped closer to the man so

he had to look up. "I hated the way I left and it took me a really long time to be okay. But I'm okay. I am."

"Son, I mean, Cam—"

"There was a time in my life when you calling me son was about the best thing I could imagine. And I wouldn't mind if you called me that again."

Oh, Max really was the waterworks these days. His eyes welled.

"I don't know if I deserve that," Max said.

"Well, I'm in charge. And I do."

Cameron smiled wide at the old man and all those years...they vanished. "Max," he said. "You look like you could use a hug."

Max's laugh was teary as Cameron pulled him in for a back-slapping hug. They hadn't been much on these when he'd been a kid. Max was a firm handshake kind of guy, not a hugger. This felt both incredibly awkward...and right.

"But I need to tell you something, Max. Or...I don't know, ask you something."

"Yeah?"

He struggled to find the right words.

Max smiled at him like he knew and then stepped away over to the shed. He threw open the door, revealing the wheelbarrow and stacks of wood.

So many years with this man doing exactly the same thing, and Cameron was suddenly so grateful that his world had come around like this. A full circle. Not just because of Josie, although lord, was he grateful for Josie. But for this family.

"Max," he said.

"I'm listening."

"I'm going to marry Josie. Maybe not this year. Or next. But I will."

Max turned, his face careful. But this time Cameron understood what that careful face meant. It wasn't judgment or censure. It was love. Love barely restrained.

"I'd like your blessing. I know Josie would, too."

The snow had started falling again and they could hear the muffled sounds of family and Alice's favorite carol on repeat.

"You have it, son. You've always had it."

JOSIE

Well, she'd messed it up. Jumped too soon. After all those years of waiting and then being separated, she'd gotten drunk on contact and made a mess of things with Cameron.

"It's snowing again," Helen said, looking out the window.

"Have you heard from Evan?" Josie asked. They were sitting on the couch cutting up pieces of paper for the big round of games that the whole family would play before dinner. Fishbowl and Empire. Another Christmas Eve tradition. They'd play games and then the youngest of the kids would go to bed up in the rooms in the lodge and the parents and grandparents would stuff the stockings and drink some wine.

Add the finishing touches the next day.

And then it would be Christmas. There would be the mayhem of the morning, but that would be over by noon. And then an afternoon of laziness and reading books and playing games that had been stuffed in stockings. And after a Herculean clean-up effort the next day the lodge would be open again to guests. The restaurant full. The holiday over.

"Last night. He got to the airport but all the highways are closed so he's still in the city."

"There's still plenty of time," Josie said. And she touched her cousin's shoulder, which was stiff and tense under her flannel shirt.

"Yeah," Helen said with a smile that did not reach her eyes. "What about you? Are you okay?"

"Fine," Josie said but Helen gave her the sympathetic look she'd just gotten from Josie.

The front door opened, letting in Max and Cameron with a blast of cold air.

The men put their backs to the door, arms full of wood, snow dusting their hair. And they were...laughing.

Max and Cameron were *laughing?*

The whole room noticed, everyone turning to stare at the two men as they carried the wood over to the fireplace and then kicked off their boots and hung up their coats. Chatting away about a summer Cameron planted trees in Northern Canada.

He's had so many lives, she thought. *So many. It's no wonder he doesn't want me. I've had one life and I've wasted it doing stupid things.*

She stood, needing some air that hadn't touched Cameron, and headed for the kitchen. Mom and Grandma Iris were in there, drinking tea or maybe whiskey in teacups. It was hard to know with those two.

"Josie," Mom said, standing up straight. "Are you all right?"

No. I've blown up my life and I'm right back where I was when I was a kid, loving Cameron and not knowing what he thinks of me.

She opened her mouth to say *fine.* To smile and maybe ask for a teacup full of whiskey, but when she opened her mouth, nothing happened. There were no words. It was like her brain was saying—*you can't do this anymore. This is no way to survive.*

"Oh honey," Iris said, and Mom got out a teacup.

"Iris is having whiskey. I'm having tea. Which do you want?"

Josie pointed to the whiskey.

"I'll be okay," she said, and she knew that was the truth. The only way to survive heartache was to just push your way through. And she hadn't done that years ago. She'd run from it and she'd been running ever since. If there was one thing she could leave this place with when Christmas was over, it was the knowledge that whatever came after this heartbreak was better than what had come before.

She felt good about that. Even if she did want to throw herself at her mom and cry.

The kitchen door opened and Cameron walked in. The storm outside had picked up its pace again and roared around the corners of the lodge like some kind of soundtrack to his entrance.

She took a sip of her whiskey and winced.

"Delia? Iris? Can you give Josie and I a second?"

Iris walked by Cameron and squeezed his hand. "I'm so happy you're back," she said, and Mom seconded that, and then they were out the door.

"Iris didn't say that to me," Josie said, trying for a joke.

"I always knew I was her favorite," Cameron said with a smile. He stepped closer and Josie, instinctively, stepped back. Cameron stopped. Stricken.

"I just...I feel like a fool. You know? And I think I just need a second before we slip right back into being friends again. I know I rushed things," she said. "Quitting my job and then trying to co-opt your work. It wasn't fair. And I'm sorry."

Cameron ran a hand through his hair and winced at her. "I think I just rushed things too," he said and then looked down at her teacup. "Is that tea or whiskey?"

"Whiskey."

"Can I—?"

She handed him the teacup and he shot it down. Josie, despite the pain and doubt, couldn't help but laugh. "You all right—?"

"I just asked Max for his blessing to marry you."

Josie stumbled backward onto a stool. "You did what?"

"I know," he said. "I mean, the words just came out. Maybe not this year. Or maybe not for a bunch of years, but you and I are getting married."

"That's what you said?"

"I did. I said that."

They gaped at each other. Until the shock of it all cleared away and made room for a wild burst of joy. She laughed and then clapped her hand over her mouth.

"I mean...what are we doing?" she asked.

He smiled the smile that made her feel like she was sitting in sunlight. The smile that made her feel seen and heard. And loved.

So loved.

"Maybe we're not rushing things," he said, slipping his fingers into her hair, cupping her face. "Maybe we're just catching up."

"I like that," she breathed. "I like you."

That made him laugh and kiss her forehead. Her nose. "I love you, Josie. I have loved you since you were sixteen years old. And I don't know what happens next. But whatever it is, I just want to be with you."

"That's exactly what I was thinking."

He kissed her, and she wrapped her arms around his

back and pulled him in close. "I love you," she breathed into his mouth. Across his skin. Over all the years they'd been together and apart. "But what if...what if we don't actually like each other? What if I snore and you're a nag? What if we're selfish—"

He shook his head, already about to prove her wrong. "We come from the same place, Josie. All those people in the other room. All those good honest, hardworking people brought us up. Showed us the way. Nothing bad has come from this place."

"The Riverview does make special people."

"None as special as you," he said.

"I think that's the whiskey talking."

"It's my heart talking," he said and kissed her again. And again.

"I have one more question for you," he said.

"Right. The always elusive fifth question."

"Will you come with me? To Australia and New Zealand. Travel. Figure out a show. Build something? Together. You an—"

"Yes. Yes. To all of it." She hugged him as hard as she could, like she could make up for all the years they'd been apart. As if she could absorb him right into her body.

"Best. Christmas. Ever." Cameron said.

EPILOGUE

Ten Months Later

"Where are we going?" Josie asked, stumbling on something and clutching at Cameron's hand. The blindfold was a little much.

"Can't you trust me?"

"I think we left trust behind with the blindfold, Cam."

"That's not what you were saying the other night," he joked, and she blushed. Ten months of sex with Cameron and her body went swimmy at just the thought of him. The idea of him. It was her own wild luck that she got to have that man in her bed all the time.

They were outdoors. She was guessing that she was in the woods because what she kept tripping over felt like tree roots. The sun was warm on the top of her head despite the cool late-October breeze blowing through the Catskills. They wore sweatshirts and running shoes. Which was kind of what they wore all the time now. Her NYC television executive wardrobe was moldering in boxes in her parents' house these days.

"One...more...step," he said and then stopped.

"Can I take off this blindfold?"

"Yeah. Here, let me help." He tugged on the blindfold, lifting it off her head, and he was standing right in front of her, so his beautiful eyes and beloved face were the only things she could see. Which was never a bad thing.

"Hi," she said and kissed him. He gave her a loud, smacking kiss and then leaned back. His eyes looked all around, like he was unable to focus. He'd been weird all day. And she thought she knew why but didn't understand why he might not want to talk about what was making him weird. They talked about *everything*. Like they had to make up for the years of silence.

"Are you all right?" she asked.

"Yeah? Why do you ask?"

"I mean, is it about the Netflix deal? Because we don't have to take it."

"No! I love the Netflix deal. The Netflix deal is perfect."

They'd made a trip out to the Riverview after their week-long stay in the city, pitching their idea for a show to Netflix and a bunch of other streaming channels. And he'd been a little strange, but she might have just been projecting her own nerves onto him. She wasn't nervous about the show or the contract with Netflix. No, she'd decided to compound the drama of the last few days by slipping a little gift for Cameron into her backpack when he asked her to go on this hike. And she was nervous about what he was going to say about the gift.

"So, where are we?" she asked, stepping back to try and see around him.

"Here." He turned sideways and she caught sight of an icy-blue lake surrounded by the muscular green shoulders of the Catskills. The lake was so clear it looked like a puddle of sky. Bright and blue.

"Oh my gosh, how pretty," she said.

"I wanted to bring you here the night of your graduation," he said. "But I got real weird about it and I always regretted that I never took you here."

"Well, better late than never," she said and pressed a kiss to his mouth. Then she stepped forward, pulling her backpack off her shoulders. *Now,* she thought. *Do it now.*

"Josie," he said, putting his arms around her from behind. "I can't tell you how happy I am. This last year has been the best year of my life."

"Me too," she whispered. Even with everything that had happened to Helen and the grief that lay over the inn like a veil, she and Cameron had managed to have real joy. "More than I ever thought possible."

"Well, once you quit that job," he said, making the same joke he'd been making all year.

"Yeah," she said. "It has nothing to do with you."

He chuckled in her ear and kissed her neck before stepping back. She pulled the box out of the backpack, clutching it to her stomach, and set the backpack down on the hard dirt.

"Cameron," she said. "I really want to ask you something."

"Me first," he said, and she turned.

And found him on one knee holding a little back box in his hands.

Oh, she thought. *Oh my.*

"Will you be my wife?"

"Well," she said, tears in her eyes. "It's funny, but I was going to ask you the same thing. I know it's not a ring, but..." She held out the box in her hand, another, newer version of the high-tech camping coffeemaker she'd gotten for him years ago. "I want to be with you on all your adventures."

He took the box from her and she opened his to find a beautiful diamond and sapphire ring. "Alice and your mom came shopping with me when they visited us in France last month."

"That's what you three snuck off to do," she breathed. "It's beautiful. It's perfect."

He pulled the ring from the box and she held out her hand. Of course it slid right onto her finger like it had been made for her. "You're perfect," she said.

"So? Is this a yes?"

"Of course it's a yes," she said. "I've loved you..." Forever. Since the moment she saw him. For most of her life. Since before she even knew him. All of those were right.

"Me too," he said, and stood and pulled her into his arms. The morning fell in beautiful golden sheets around them. And it felt like a benediction. A prayer. A holy agreement that they were the right two people for this promise.

"I brought some coffee," she said. "To make in the coffeemaker. A toast...I mean, it seems a little ridiculous compared to this ring." God, it really did glitter and shine in the sunlight. Had there ever been a more perfect ring?

"Come on," he said, linking their fingers. "I know a perfect spot."

And she went with him, right by his side, because for the rest of her life, the best spot for her was right by his side.

HEY READERS—THANK you so much for picking up *Christmas at the Riverview Inn*. Cameron and Josie have been waiting a long time for their HEA—I hope it was worth it. Now, I have a sneak peek at Helen's book for you, but I have to warn you, it starts with heartache. So if you want to hold on to your Christmas happily ever after glow—maybe turn the page another time. But if you're intrigued (and ready for a little heartbreak) go ahead and read a sample of *Second Chance at the Riverview Inn.*

SECOND CHANCE AT THE RIVERVIEW INN

HELEN

The light outside the window was purple. The color of a bruise. It wasn't dawn. Not yet. But it was coming. Christmas Day.

And something was wrong.

Very wrong.

Helen ran a hand over her belly and felt the flutter of the baby. The popcorn pop of him or her kicking and moving.

The baby is fine.

So what's wrong?

Josie and Cameron were back at the Riverview, and they hadn't been able to keep their hands off each other the previous night. Helen was taking that as a good sign they had put the past behind them and were getting a second chance at the love they deserved.

And she'd very cheerfully taken credit for that at every opportunity.

So, it wasn't missing Josie or Cameron that was wrong.

What was it?

Her phone, which she'd put on her chest, buzzed and her heart leaped when she checked it.

It was just some junk email. Just like it had been all night long.

Her heart was sore from jumping every time her phone binged. Her eyes were gritty from lack of sleep and she was...she was sick to her stomach. In a way she hadn't been for weeks.

She tapped her messages icon and read the last thing Evan had written last night.

Break in storm. I've rented a car. I'll see you soon.

He should have been here by midnight. One at the latest. But there'd been no word. She'd sent a dozen texts. Called every ten minutes. Nothing. His phone went immediately to voice mail. She imagined he'd left the charger in his bag, which was undoubtedly in the trunk of the car. So his phone might be dead.

And she imagined that the break in the storm he'd seen in New York City had vanished as soon as he headed up the Hudson, and he'd pulled over into any one of the hotels that were open on Christmas Eve.

Evan had been working and traveling nonstop, so he'd probably hit that bed and fallen hard asleep.

All of that made perfect sense.

But something was really wrong. And she felt it deep in her chest where all the true things she knew about herself lived.

She got out of bed and pulled on her sweatpants and one of Evan's sweatshirts, the big, thick Boston College Crew one that he always wanted back and she refused to return.

Evan, she thought and then she prayed it.

Please, Evan. Please.

It was four in the morning. A cold and quiet time. The

fire had burned to embers and the heat it had been pumping out all evening had disappeared. She stirred the embers the way Max had taught all of them, laying down kindling and blowing on the tiny flames until they caught. Soon the fire was crackling and sending out sparks.

The Christmas tree had been unplugged, probably by Alice, so Helen got on her hands and knees and plugged it back in, and then crawled out from under the tree, with pine needles in her hair.

"Helen?"

"Hey Mom." She got to her feet and turned to see her mother standing at the bottom of the big staircase. She wore leggings and a flannel shirt. Her hair, the kind of silver blond women paid a gazillion dollars for, was in a messy ponytail. "What are you doing up?"

"I don't know. I just had a strange feeling." Her mother rubbed her chest. That same place where Helen felt the heavy certainty that something was wrong. "Evan must have gotten in late."

"He's not here yet."

They blinked at each other. And Helen knew, the way she always knew with her mother, that they were thinking the same thing.

Something is wrong.

"Well," Mom said with false cheer. "I hope he's not at that terrible Motel 8 in Binghampton. Because that's the—"

There was a heavy knock on the door. The kind of knock that didn't bring good cheer and glad tidings.

Not at four a.m. Not on Christmas Day.

It was the kind of knock that changed everything. That drew a line down the middle of a life. Before and after.

"Helen," Mom whispered and reached for her, grabbing her hands just when Helen thought she might pass out.

Another knock. Louder.

"We need to get it before everyone wakes up."

Helen crossed to the door, feeling the chill grow the further she got from the fire. The closer she got to whatever was going to happen next.

Mom was beside her and that was good. Helen felt like she was watching the whole thing from a million miles away. Like looking through the wrong end of a telescope, so instead of large and close everything was tiny and distant.

She pulled open the door and there was a State Trooper in his full foul-weather gear. His nose and cheeks were pink from the wind.

It was a bad storm. That's what I'll say about tonight, she thought. *That's how the story will go that I'll tell my baby. It was a really bad storm.*

"Sorry to bother you ma'am," he said and took off his hat.

Don't, she wanted to say. *You'll get cold.*

"I'm looking for Helen Larson," he said.

"That's me," she whispered and put a hand over her belly like she might protect the baby from what was about to happen. The State Trooper saw the gesture, realized she was pregnant, and closed his eyes like he, too, was praying.

Tears were falling down her face, because she knew. She knew in her chest where all the sure things lived for her.

"There's been an accident," he said. "A tractor trailer lost control on the highway just outside Binghampton."

"Evan Daniels?" she asked. *I was going to be Helen Daniels. And we joked that if we had a boy we'd call him Daniel and he'd hate us, but also might be a country music singer.*

"I'm sorry, ma'am. He died on the way to the hospital."

And she'd known. She'd known so well and so

completely that this was the thing wrong. That Evan was gone, that it wasn't even shocking.

But the world went black all the same.

SECOND CHANCE at The Riverview Inn will be out in May. Join my newsletter for updates. Or follow me on facebook! Or Bookbub for updates!